Ryan Quinn and the
Rebel's Escape

RYAN
QUINN
AND THE REBEL'S ESCAPE

RON McGEE

HARPER
An Imprint of HarperCollinsPublishers

Ryan Quinn and the Rebel's Escape
Text copyright © 2016 by Ron McGee
Illustrations copyright © 2016 by Chris Samnee

Library of Congress Control Number: 2016936058
ISBN 978-0-06-242164-7

Book design by Victor Joseph Ochoa
16 17 18 19 20   CG/RRDH   10 9 8 7 6 5 4 3 2 1
❖
First Edition

Life is full of daring adventures.
But they're a lot more fun if you have
amazing people to share them with.
So thanks to Mom, Dad, and Brian for
all the great adventures growing up.
And thanks to Eufe, Alex, and Claudia
for all the journeys we still have in
front of us.

—RM

PROLOGUE

**NANSANG PROVINCE,
ANDAKAR**

Lan was only sixteen and about to die.

The Army Services Intelligence agents were narrowing the distance, getting closer every second. Struggling up the steep hill, Lan glanced back, fighting exhaustion and fear. The jungle was dense here, and moonlight broke through only sporadically. The flashlight beams of the ASI agents in pursuit bounced wildly back and forth.

Slipping on wet leaves, Lan stumbled, dangerously close to tumbling back down the steep incline. At the last possible moment, a powerful hand reached out and grabbed hold.

"We just have to make it to the temple. You can do it," the American said. In the gloom, his face was all hard lines and shadows, but there was determination in his eyes. Lan didn't want to disappoint him after he'd risked so much in getting them both to safety. Supporting each other, they made it over the last rise of the hill and onto the open plateau up top.

The grounds of the Mae Wong Temples appeared ghostly in the moonlight. Abandoned for two thousand years, these ancient ruins remained strictly off-limits to tourists. Forty years ago, when this country's military regime seized power, Mae Wong was the site of a bloody massacre of Buddhist priests. It remained a potent symbol of rebellion that Lan had often dreamed of visiting. But not like this. Not just to become yet another victim of the brutal government's soldiers.

"There," the American said, pointing to a small structure about thirty yards to their left. "The hiding place is inside that stupa, the one with the golden dome."

Lan looked back at the flashlights bouncing their way up the hill. "They're right behind us."

"We'll be safe inside the temple. Come on— we're almost there."

Lan wanted to believe it was true. After all the months of secrecy and risk, the constant fear of being discovered, would it finally be over? Could this stranger actually save them? Suddenly, an explosive blast shattered the night and the American jerked forward as a bullet ripped into him. Blood splattered Lan's cheek.

Watching the American fall to the ground, Lan knew that now all hope was lost.

PART ONE

WHAT YOU DON'T KNOW CAN HURT YOU

CHAPTER
01

**NEW YORK,
USA**

No more fights.

The promise he'd made to his mother ran through Ryan Quinn's mind as he stood in the school hallway. Drew Stieglitz, a junior and the starting center on the basketball team, shoved Ryan's friend Danny into the metal lockers. Stieglitz was a full head taller than Danny, with a square jaw, giant hands, and the swagger of a guy used to getting his way.

"I told you to leave her alone." Stieglitz slammed Danny into the locker once again for emphasis.

"I thought that was more of a suggestion," Danny said. Short and slim, with spiky black hair and a cocky grin, Danny had a never-ending supply of manic energy. He showed no fear, but Ryan knew his friend was sweating.

Stieglitz leaned in close. "Keep it up, you little dwarf, you're gonna get your butt kicked."

"For talking to a gorgeous girl?" Danny glanced at Kasey, Stieglitz's beautiful and popular little sister, who watched with an alarmed expression. "Gotta tell you, Steeg, even a butt-kicking from you sounds worth it."

A few of the students who had gathered around laughed at Danny's confident attitude.

"Drew, chill," Kasey said, putting a hand on her brother's arm to calm him. She was in two of Ryan's classes, but they'd talked only once. Well, actually *she'd* talked and Ryan had just sort of nodded and stared. And then felt so embarrassed that he couldn't even look at her again.

"Stay out of it." Stieglitz shrugged her off, focused on Danny. "You've a real smart mouth. Think you're funny."

"I'm guessing you're not a fan." Danny tried to sound tough, but his nerves were starting to get the better of him. He looked at Ryan, hoping for some backup.

"You're about to find out," Stieglitz said.

No more fights.

Ryan had been at his new school here in New York for more than two months without any problems. Almost a record for him lately. He'd been in trouble for fighting several times over the last year. The worst was when his family was living in Ghana for a few months. A couple of English teens, tourists visiting Africa with a school group, were throwing rocks at kids from a local village and calling them names. Ryan just wanted them to stop, but things got out of hand. One of the boys ended up with a broken nose, the other with his arm in a sling, and Ryan got hauled off by the police. Luckily, his dad was able to talk the cops into letting him go with a warning.

There were other fights, too. Ryan had a bad habit of getting pulled into other people's problems. It was like he couldn't help himself. Here in New York, though, things were finally going well—really well, actually. And the last thing he wanted was for anything to screw that up.

Like getting dragged into this. But what was he supposed to do, stand by and watch Danny get beaten to a pulp?

Ryan stepped forward. "Let him go."

Stieglitz gave Ryan a dismissive glance, then looked back to his two buddies behind him.

"Did somebody dose all the eighth graders with stupid pills this year?"

"He was just talking to her. Kasey's in a couple of classes with us." Ryan moved in closer, his tone relaxed but making it clear that he wasn't backing away. "No big deal."

Stieglitz turned to face him. Ryan could tell that the jock was keenly aware that people were watching.

"She's my sister. I'll decide what's a big deal," Stieglitz said. Stieglitz shifted position, zeroing in on his new target. Ryan kept his expression neutral, but watched Stieglitz closely, searching for a sign of his intentions.

Stieglitz's first swing was a respectably fast sucker punch, coming in high and from the right. Ryan instinctively dodged, keeping his body weight balanced on the toes of his left foot as he pivoted out of the way. The momentum of the swing threw Stieglitz off-balance and he barely stopped himself from falling. Ryan had a clear shot, but he held back. He didn't want to hit the other boy unless he absolutely had to.

Stieglitz glanced back at his friends. "Kick his butt, Steeg," one of them said, inching forward.

"I don't want to do this," Ryan said. "I kinda

promised my mom I wouldn't get into any fights."

"Should've thought about your mommy before you opened your mouth." Stieglitz shot forward, trying to grab Ryan's well-worn Psychedelic Furs T-shirt with hands that could easily palm a basketball. Ryan stepped back, once more shifting away from the bigger kid so that he missed and stumbled.

"Whoosh—all air! And the crowd goes wild!" Danny said, beaming as Kasey's friends laughed.

Ryan glared at Danny.

"What?" Danny was all innocence.

Students drifted closer, smelling blood in the air and wanting a ringside seat. Stieglitz spun around, angry at being made to look stupid.

"Drew, come on—lay off," Kasey said. She glanced at her brother and then looked anxiously at Ryan. Was she actually worried for him—or did she just think he was nuts for taking on her brother? Ryan couldn't quite tell.

"Big mistake," Stieglitz growled.

Ryan managed to pull his eyes away from Kasey's just in time. Stieglitz charged, determined to ram him into the lockers. Ryan sidestepped with the smooth moves of a dancer. The bigger boy's lack of control would be his downfall. Stieglitz whizzed past and Ryan tapped his shoulder just enough to throw his balance off. Stieglitz crashed into the metal lockers with the force of a bull.

A collective groan went up from the watching students as they heard skull hit metal. Stieglitz dropped to the ground, dazed, as the fourth-period bell rang. Everyone scattered, excited to spread word of how Stieglitz was beaten by a kid half his size.

"That was awesome," Danny whispered to Ryan. "Stupid and probably suicidal—but definitely awesome."

"Mr. Quinn."

Ryan and Danny whirled around to find Principal Milankovic staring at them. The hall cleared quickly as students made themselves scarce. Ryan noticed Kasey's friends grab her by the arm and pull her away. Stieglitz took one look at the principal, then lurched to his feet and stumbled off as well.

"My office, Mr. Quinn," the principal said.

Ryan's shoulders slumped. "I barely even *touched* him."

"Now."

CHAPTER

02

NEW YORK, USA

The International Community School of New York was only six blocks from the United Nations Headquarters and had a student body that included kindergartners all the way up to high school seniors. Many of the kids who attended were the sons and daughters of UN employees. Ryan's algebra class alone had a Saudi Arabian prince, the Minister of Thailand's daughter, and a Somali refugee whose mother was on the Human Rights committee.

It was a perfect fit for Ryan, whose father, John, worked as a director for the United Nations Development Programme. Until recently, Ryan had spent most of his life as a nomad, traveling from place to place. His dad was stationed for a year or two at a time in different countries, and the family had lived all over the world.

When he was younger, Ryan enjoyed living in unusual places. He made friends with local kids pretty easily and each place offered some cool new experience—hide-and-seek in a forest in Belarus, paddleboarding off the coast of Nicaragua, ice fishing in Norway. He never had time to get bored anywhere because they'd soon be off to someplace different.

Out of necessity, Ryan learned to adapt. He studied local kids closely for clues on how to act and then imitated them, becoming good at blending in. He'd change the clothes he wore, the expressions he used, the foods he ate. Whatever made him fit in. Language wasn't much of a barrier when he was young, especially among boys who could occupy themselves for hours playing sports and games.

But as he got older, fitting in was harder. Kids already had their group of friends and weren't as quick to talk to the new guy. Ryan had become something of a chameleon, able to change with each new environment, but he didn't feel like he belonged anywhere. He was always on the outside looking in.

More and more, he just hung out alone. He'd get home from whatever school he was attending and go to his room. Some days, he'd practice the magic tricks his dad taught him when he was growing up, or maybe play guitar. He'd read until his eyes glazed over, then put headphones on and listen to music.

His room became his refuge. Though the location changed every time they moved, one thing was the same: his awesome collection of baseball caps always hung proudly on the wall. Ryan had caps from every Major League team in America. He'd started collecting them when he was eleven and his parents took him to a Washington Nationals game. It was on one of their trips "home," as they called it. Which was totally weird to Ryan since he'd never lived in the States for more than a month or two at a time.

After that trip, though, he started thinking about living in the United States a lot. What would it be like to go to a backyard barbecue and wolf down hot dogs and hamburgers? Or to watch a Friday night football game with cheerleaders and a marching band? Or grow up with the same set of friends who'd known you for more than a few months? Every baseball cap

Ryan added to his collection made him feel a little more connected to an America he knew mostly through books and movies.

That's when the fights started. Ryan insisted to his mom and dad that there was always a good reason: A younger kid was being teased or some bully was picking on Ryan. Kids could be jerks in every country around the world. But secretly, Ryan knew it was more than that. Sometimes, he just felt like he was crawling out of his skin, like he was keeping all this stuff inside that needed some way to get out. The fights didn't really make him feel better, but they kept happening.

One night, he overheard his parents arguing. Ryan's dad thought the moodiness and acting out was normal, just a teenage boy growing up. But his mom understood how unhappy Ryan really was. Their work was starting to hurt Ryan, she told his dad. He needed to plant roots, to make friends. He needed a home. As Ryan sat behind the wall listening, he realized she was right. What he wanted more than anything was to just be a normal American kid with a normal, boring life.

It took a while to work everything out, but now he finally had what he'd been dreaming of:

a home in New York City (which had *two* base-ball teams, the Mets and the Yankees!), a school where he felt like he could finally just be himself, and a best friend he could really talk to.

Everything he'd wanted—and he was about to lose it all.

Principal Milankovic glared at Ryan from under bushy eyebrows. "You understand that fighting is grounds for immediate dismissal?" For a school principal, he was surprisingly big, with massive arms and a barrel chest that made him look more like an aging boxer than a high school principal.

"Yes, sir."

"That's all? You're not going to tell me he started it? That it was self-defense or something?" The principal's Slavic accent was noticeable.

"Would it matter if I did?"

Principal Milankovic smiled. "No, it would not."

Milankovic came around his massive desk, overflowing with stacks of paper piled haphazardly. "Our actions have consequences. The reasons for those actions may be sound; you may be justified in what you choose to do. But you will still have to deal with the consequences of those choices."

Ryan didn't meet Milankovic's eyes, his gut twisted in knots. If he made it through this without getting kicked out of school, he promised himself he'd stay out of the fight next time—no more risking his own neck, even for a friend like Danny.

Sitting next to him, Milankovic shifted his tone and said, "Your grandfather understood about consequences."

Ryan's head jerked up, meeting the principal's steady gaze. "You knew my grandfather?"

"A little. He was an extraordinary man. I was sorry to hear of his passing."

"How did you know him?"

"He did me a great favor once, many years ago."

"What kind of favor?"

For a moment, Milankovic looked thoughtful, his mind far away. Then his eyes snapped back to Ryan's as he dismissed whatever memories had flooded in, stern once more. "You do not fight in my school. Understood?"

Ryan nodded. "I won't—I promise."

"And I know the Quinns always keep their

promises." He stood up. "Get to class. And don't let me see you in here again."

Ryan jumped up and hurried out before the principal could change his mind.

CHAPTER 03

NEW YORK, USA

Ryan saw Danny bouncing down the front stairs toward him as school let out. "Where'd you learn to do that? You were like a ghost—one second you were there and the next you were gone."

"It's just something my dad taught me," Ryan said, acting like it wasn't a big deal. "We lived in some pretty dangerous places. He wanted me to be able to defend myself."

"Can you, like, kill people and stuff?"

"Yeah, but I've only had to do that a couple of times."

Danny stopped on the bottom step, looking back, eyes wide. "Seriously?"

Ryan grinned. "Dude—really?"

"Jerk." Danny was grinning, too.

Actually, Ryan did know how to knock some-body out or break some bones, if he had to. But the last thing he needed was getting a rep as a good fighter. He knew from experience that was a sure way to invite more trouble.

The front of the school was crowded with limos and bodyguards waiting to pick up the kids of dignitaries. Ryan and Danny navigated the black-suited security guards who refused to move out of the way, their cold stares slightly vacant as students flowed around them on all sides.

"Can you teach me how to do some of that ninja stuff?" Danny said.

"Sure—you'd be good at it."

"Course I would—I'm small and fast. Makes me harder to hit."

Danny made Ryan laugh a lot. They had met during Ryan's first week at ICS. Sitting next to each other in physical science class, Danny noticed Ryan's shirt, a vintage concert tee from The Smiths's *Meat Is Murder* tour, and they started talking '80s alt-rock bands. Danny was a die-hard fan of The Cure, and they got absorbed in a debate on which was the better band—a debate that nearly got them both a detention.

Picking up the conversation after school, they didn't stop talking for hours. They'd ended up hanging out at Danny's apartment for so long that Danny's mom invited Ryan for dinner. The family was originally from the Philippine Islands, and they were all shocked when Ryan said how much he loved *kare-kare* stew and rice with *bagoong*. After Ryan said "thank you" in Tagalog—the Filipino language—they practically made him an honorary member of the family.

Since then, Ryan and Danny had hung out often. Both were outsiders in their own way: Danny was a techno-geek who often tried too hard to make people like him, and Ryan felt like his new American school was as unfamiliar as any of the foreign countries where he'd lived. But with Danny, Ryan didn't feel like he had to try and blend in. He could just be himself. Who-ever that was. Ryan was still figuring it out.

"Ryan, Danny—wait up!" a girl's voice called. The guys turned, surprised to see Kasey Stieg-litz pushing through the crowd, joining them at the bottom of the steps.

"Hey, Kasey, what's going on?" Danny greeted Kasey as if it was totally normal for the prettiest girl in the eighth grade to be heading over. Ryan didn't know what it was about Kasey that turned him into a mumbling idiot. It's not like he couldn't talk to girls. He wasn't nearly as smooth as Danny, but he wasn't terrible (at least, he didn't *think* so). But something about Kasey, with her wild, unruly hair and her casual confidence, threw him completely off his game.

"Sorry about Drew," Kasey said. "I told him to stop acting like a jerk."

Danny shrugged. "He doesn't bother us. I just hope we don't have to teach him a lesson again."

Kasey smiled, glancing at Ryan. He just grinned back. And kicked himself inwardly. Talk, he begged himself.

"Which way you going?" Kasey asked.

"Up to the Rose," Danny said. "You?"

"Downtown—got this meeting. Guess I'll see you in class."

As she turned to leave, Ryan blurted out, "Actually, I'm going downtown."

"Yeah?" Kasey said, turning back.

"I help out at my mom's store."

"Mind if I walk with you?"

"I—no—that's . . ."

Danny rolled his eyes. "He'd love it."

Kasey lit up. "Great—let me just tell Lisa so she doesn't wait. Be right back."

As she darted away, Danny whacked Ryan playfully in the chest. "She's totally into you."

"What? No . . ."

"Trust me. I know about these things."

Ryan watched Kasey as she told her friends the new plans and then bounded back toward them. The girls glanced at Ryan, whispering and grinning, the gossip machine shifting into over-drive.

"Dude, kill the smile—you're so obvious," Danny said.

"Shut up." Ryan did, however, do his best to seem cool as Kasey returned.

"Ready?" she said.

Danny backed away. "You two have fun."

Ryan glared at him, but Danny only winked, then disappeared into the crowd.

"He's funny," Kasey said, watching Danny. "Like he stepped out of an anime comic or something."

"He'd consider that high praise."

As they started walking, Ryan was a little nervous that Stieglitz might be watching them together and come after him to start another fight. He scanned the area for trouble and sud-denly stopped. Behind an SUV across the street, a man in a dark suit was looking in their direction. Though he was pretty far away, it seemed to Ryan as if the man was staring right at him.

"Coming?" Kasey asked, now a few steps ahead.

"Yeah." When he looked back across the street, the man had disappeared.

CHAPTER
04

**NEW YORK,
USA**

yan and Kasey walked along 37th Street, the crisp November air chilly against their light jackets. Determined not to let his nerves get the better of him, Ryan reached inside his jacket pocket for his secret weapon—chocolate.

No matter how different and unusual Ryan found the cultures of the places he'd lived around the world, one thing had always been constant. People loved chocolate. Kids loved it. Adults loved it. And Ryan kind of obsessed over it. He'd had rich, dark chocolate in Belgium; milk chocolate with curry powder in India; even *xocolatl*, the thick chocolate drink made with hot chilies and adored by the Aztecs a thousand years ago. Chocolate was the ultimate icebreaker.

Stopping at the light, he held out several small, brightly wrapped bars to Kasey. "Want one?"

"Thanks. Are they all different?"

Ryan pointed to one in a green wrapper that was long and thin. "This one's from Switzerland—it's just a plain ganache with a cocoa-nib crust. Simple, but delicious. The blue one's from Ecuador. They grow all their cacao beans in the same place they make the bars. Which is very unusual. And the one in gold is chocolate mixed with bacon. Sounds gross, but it's incredible. The chocolatier trained at Le Cordon Bleu in Paris. Only uses the highest-quality ingredients."

Kasey laughed. "You're kind of a chocolate snob, aren't you?"

Ryan could tell her teasing was playful. "I try it everywhere I go. And I've been a lot of places."

"So which should I choose?"

Ryan handed her the one in green. "This one. They make the bars in Zurich, but all the cacao beans are grown on this farm in Cameroon close to where I lived for a while."

The light changed and they started walking as Kasey unwrapped her small chocolate bar. "You lived in Cameroon?" she asked. "Were you there during the education protests last year?"

Ryan looked at her in surprise. "You know about that?"

"I watched videos that were posted online. All those students coming together, standing up for themselves. I wish I could have seen it." She bit into her chocolate bar. "Oh my god—*so* good."

"Right?"

"Did you see any of the protests?"

Most of the kids Ryan met here in the States didn't know a lot about what was going on around the world, much less in a small country in Africa. But Kasey actually seemed interested.

"I was in one."

Kasey stopped short. "No way. Like, really *in* it?"

"A group of students passed right by our school," he told her. "It was mostly young people, and so some of us just joined in. The leaders wanted to block this bridge. We piled up all these tires and things so no one could cross."

"Sounds like the French Revolution when they built those barricades."

"That's what it felt like. Traffic piled up in every direction. The whole city came to a standstill. Eventually, these cops came in with tear gas and machine guns. Everybody just ran. It was chaos."

"You got gassed?" She sounded half-horrified, half-thrilled at the thought.

"A little—my throat felt like it was on fire for hours."

"That's incredible."

"It was. Scary, too." The truth was, Ryan got in over his head before he realized just how crazy the situation would get. Looting and vandalism. Smoke everywhere. Ryan was swept along, enjoying the feeling that he was part of something bigger, that his actions had some purpose and might make a difference. But the protests became more violent as the police cracked down. One of his classmates, a German girl he studied with sometimes, was hit by a cop's baton and dropped to the ground. She was bleeding as Ryan fought through the crowd and pulled her back to safety.

"In the end," Ryan said, "we didn't do much good. Nothing really changed."

"At least you tried."

"People got hurt. I still don't know if it was worth it."

Ryan had never talked to anyone about that day, not even his parents. He was afraid they'd be angry with him for putting himself in danger. Talking to Kasey, though, came easily. "How did you hear about it?"

Kasey gave him a half smile. "I do have some idea of what's going on in the world."

"Sorry, I didn't mean—"

"I'm kidding. I got interested when I was in this bizarre little theater piece last semester."

"You act?" Ryan asked.

Kasey nodded. "Yeah, and the school brought in this Romanian director who was brilliant but totally crazy. The play was all about revolution with real-life characters from all these different time periods—Roman slaves, French peasants, George Washington. It was so insane."

Ryan loved Kasey's laugh. "I wish I could've seen it."

"It was pretty terrible. But it got me interested in things in a way I'd never really been before. I've been reading a lot more history since then, watching more news. Some of it's just so sad, though," she said. "It's like you said. It feels like all this bad stuff is going on and there's not much we can do to help."

As they turned the corner onto Lexington, Kasey stopped in the doorway of an older office building. "Well, this is where my meeting is."

"What kind of meeting?"

"Don't laugh." Kasey took a piece of paper from a folder she carried, handing it to Ryan. It was a flyer that read: "Books Not Bombs!" She continued, "We're trying to get the government to spend more money on schools and education instead of on making weapons. You can come, if you want."

"I promised my mom I'd help her out. Maybe next time?"

"Sure." Kasey pushed the glass door to go inside, but Ryan stepped forward, holding it open for her. "Thanks." She suddenly seemed nervous as she blurted out, "I don't suppose you have any interest in going to the Autumn Carnival Dance on Saturday?"

"Um, I've never really done much dancing."

"Don't worry, I'm a klutz. We can trip over each other's feet."

Ryan forced himself not to smile like a dork. "Sure," he said, "It'll be my first official dance."

"Great!" Kasey started inside. "Oh, you might want to avoid my brother. He's not as horrible as he seems, but he can be protective."

"I got that."

Grinning, Ryan watched her walk away. When she disappeared into the stairwell, he finally stepped back, letting go of the door. As it slowly closed, Ryan froze.

Through the reflection in the glass, Ryan could see across the street directly behind him. The man in the dark suit from the school was there again, staring right at him.

CHAPTER

05

NEW YORK, USA

Ryan fought his initial instinct to turn and stare. Instead, he started down the street at a brisk pace, believing that the stranger was probably watching his movements closely. His parents had warned him about being careful in the places they lived, but he'd thought New York would be safe by comparison.

Ryan took out his cell phone and held it up, thumbs moving over the keys as though he was texting somebody. He held the phone awkwardly, raising it slightly over his shoulder so the camera had a good vantage point behind him.

Click—click—click.

Ryan spun the phone around and pulled up the photos he'd just taken. The man kept several people between them at all times. His gaze, however, never wavered, focused like a laser on Ryan's back. He was of Asian descent, medium height with military-short black hair and a mouth that turned down at the corners in a perpetual frown. Ryan guessed he was probably from Southeast Asia somewhere, maybe Indonesia or Thailand.

Moving quickly, Ryan tried to put some distance between them. He turned at Park Avenue, using the busier street to shake his stalker. Darting in and out of the crowd, he hunched down so the man couldn't see him as easily.

Just before the light changed, Ryan dashed across the street toward the median, which was landscaped with trees and long rows of bushes. Ryan slipped behind the greenery. At the corner, the man was forced to stop as traffic whizzed past. He pulled out a phone and dialed, then began talking via a Bluetooth earpiece, continuing to search for some sign of Ryan.

Watching, Ryan was reminded of the times he and his father had played "Follow-the-Monkey," their own version of "Follow-the-Leader." The follower was supposed to stay hidden and the monkey could go anywhere he wanted. Once, when they were in a crowded market in Rio de

Janeiro, Ryan had done so well staying hidden that his dad had panicked, thinking he'd actually lost his son.

The light changed and the stranger darted across the street, passing the bushes where Ryan was hidden. Halfway across, he stopped and whirled around, his eyes locked on the median, scanning with a professionalism that revealed he was used to tracking. Ryan's impulse was to jump and run again. Instead, he remained still. He recognized that quick turn as a classic misdirection technique. The man was becoming desperate, trying to spook his prey into moving too soon.

A yellow cab honked, zooming toward the man as the light changed once more. He jumped out of the way, hurrying to the other side. At the far corner, he looked in all directions, frustrated at having lost his target, and finally started moving down Park Avenue.

Ryan decided to turn the tables and play a little "Follow-the-Monkey" himself. As the light changed once again, Ryan joined the crowd, pulling off his green jacket and turning it inside out so the black lining showed. He opened his backpack and pulled out one of the baseball caps from his collection: a 1996 World Series

Champions commemorative hat he always kept handy. He assumed the man had tracked him by the green of his jacket and that in the black jacket and cap, he looked different enough to go unnoticed. Blending in came easily to Ryan.

The man was at the far end of the block and Ryan hurried to catch up, keeping his head low and his body hidden as much as possible. When the man stopped and turned around once more, Ryan ducked into the doorway of a bagel shop just in time, flattening his body against the wall.

He forced himself to count to five slowly, his body poised to fight if the man came after him. Reaching five, he peered out. The man was just turning onto 40th Street. Ryan darted out of his hiding place in pursuit, but as he rounded the corner, he stopped short—his follower had doubled back and was about to collide with him.

Ryan veered at the last moment, their shoulders barely missing one another. Luckily, the man was too focused on his phone conversation to notice. He had a deep, guttural voice, and he was angry. Ryan had been right. The man was speaking a Southeast Asian language, though Ryan didn't recognize this one.

As he passed, Ryan distinctly heard the man say "John Quinn." Ryan couldn't help himself.

All his self-control went out the window as he turned to stare from under his Yankees cap, shocked to hear his father's name. Just then, a black Lincoln Town Car screeched to a halt at the curb. The man yanked open the back door and climbed inside.

Ryan wanted to shout, to stop the guy and find out how he knew his dad. On the car's bumper, he recognized the red, white, and blue of a diplomatic license plate. The man tailing him was probably connected to one of the embassies in New York. Ryan snapped a picture of the plate with his phone as the Town Car sped away.

CHAPTER

06

NEW YORK, USA

Jacqueline Quinn held the violin delicately, as if it were made of glass. Her customer marveled at the rare instrument as she explained its provenance. "This one was designed by Giovanni Francesco Pressenda around 1841. The back is made of spruce."

"It's stunning," the man said.

Across the shop, Ryan watched his mother, always impressed by her deep knowledge of the instruments she sold. Jacqueline had a reverence for these musical gems that she conveyed to her customers. It's why they sought her out, no matter where she happened to be living. After all their travels, Ryan figured his mom probably knew just about every person who bought or sold musical instruments around the world. She'd been a consultant for serious collectors and auction houses, but this was the first time she'd been able to open her own shop.

Jacqueline had designed the store with counters made of rich mahogany and beveled glass. It was like a time machine back to the 1800s. She'd even somehow imported the musty aroma of old wood and pipe tobacco.

"Don't be fooled by its appearance," Jacqueline said, her slight French accent adding an essence of sophistication. "What makes this violin so exceptional is what it can *do*. Deep, resonant tones. A purity that blends the best of the Italian and French styles. It may be beautiful on the outside, but the music it produces is what makes it extraordinary."

Ryan spent a lot of afternoons here since they'd moved to New York, helping his mom unpack all the instruments and get the shop organized. Ryan found it kind of boring, but he got paid. Soon, he'd earn enough for the autographed Yogi Berra Mets hat he wanted.

Jacqueline noticed Ryan in the doorway to the back room and instantly recognized that he was upset about something. He didn't want to worry her, so he ducked back into the office and storeroom behind the store. As he left, he heard the customer ask his mother, "And how much is it?"

"One hundred and fifty thousand dollars," she answered, her calm tone making the huge number sound completely reasonable.

Ryan sat at his mom's desk, automatically reaching for the box of chocolate truffles she always kept handy. Chocolate helped him think, and right now that's exactly what he needed to do. He'd clearly heard the man say his father's name—was his dad in some kind of trouble? John Quinn had left on one of his trips two weeks earlier. He was in Thailand for a plastics trade conference. They'd talked on the phone four days ago. John told Ryan he'd be home in time to go ice-skating in Central Park this weekend. That was the last they'd heard from him. Which was strange, Ryan realized, because his dad usually checked in pretty regularly.

Out front, Ryan heard the entry-door chimes ring as the customer left. He expected his mother to check on him, but then heard more voices— somebody else must have come in. Something in Jacqueline's tone caught his attention. Though he couldn't make out the words, he could tell her voice was strained. Something was wrong.

Ryan moved to the doorway that joined the two spaces. The door was cracked open, but as he approached he kept himself partially hidden. He didn't know exactly why he did this; his mom never cared if he listened when she spoke with customers. But some instinct had kicked in, making him cautious. Nearing the door, he heard a man's voice, gruff and abrupt.

". . . You realize that lying to us could have serious consequences," he said.

"Why would I lie to you?" Jacqueline said, sounding bolder—and louder—than normal.

"Mrs. Quinn, we're only trying to help." Ryan craned his neck, peering into the shop. His mother stood in front of a man and woman, both in business suits. The man had gray hair and hard eyes; the woman was African American and tall. "When was the last time you heard from your husband?"

"A few days ago. He called from Bangkok."

"From the International Plastics Exhibition?" the woman said, consulting her notes.

"That's right. Has something happened? Why is the Central Intelligence Agency interested in John?"

The *CIA*? Ryan thought about the Asian man following him. He could have been CIA, too; but then, why the diplomatic plates on his car? And why was he coming after Ryan?

"Agent Calloway, show her the photos," the man said

The woman pulled out a packet of eight-by-ten photographs. Ryan couldn't see the pictures from where he stood, but Jacqueline glanced down and he could tell that she recognized his father. Even from a distance, Ryan could see the tension in her expression.

"These pictures were taken five days ago in Muang Tak, Thailand," the man continued. "Nowhere near Bangkok. The man there with your husband, he's a known smuggler. Muang Tak is his base of operation."

Jacqueline met the agent's stony gaze, and Ryan knew she was over her initial surprise. Her tone was calmer and more under control. "Are you accusing him of something? John meets with hundreds, maybe thousands, of people every year."

"We want to know why he's meeting with a known felon over two hundred miles from where he was supposed to be." He snatched one of the photos from Agent Calloway's hand, pushing it at Jacqueline. "It'll be a lot better for you if you tell us everything you know, Mrs. Quinn."

"I don't know anything about it at all." Ryan could tell his mother was lying—and so could the CIA agents.

"You sure this is how you want to play it?" Agent Calloway said.

"I don't know what to tell you. I'm sure John will straighten it all out."

The two agents shared a look, then turned away. The entrance chimes tinkled as the gray-haired agent opened the door and walked out.

Agent Calloway followed, but suddenly spun around. Across the room, her eyes locked on Ryan. She coolly scrutinized him and nodded her head slightly. Calloway had been aware of his presence all along, and she wanted Ryan to know it.

Drifting back to the desk, Ryan's head was spinning as he sank down into the chair. His father, a criminal? It wasn't possible—but then, why was he meeting with smugglers? And why was his mother lying about what she knew?

Jacqueline came into the back room, all the fight gone out of her. Ryan could see how worried she really was.

"Mom, what's going on?"

"Nothing. Just a mix-up, that's all." She gently brushed her son's hair off his forehead, something she'd done since he was a child.

"Where is Dad? Why hasn't he called?"

"I don't know. I'm sure he's fine," she said. Ryan stared at her, his mind reeling, because one thing had just become clear to him as he heard that louder, bolder tone creep into her voice: *His mother was lying to him, too.*

CHAPTER
07

**NEW YORK,
USA**

The scariest moment in Ryan's life had been three years ago. They were living in a town in Paraguay where Ryan's dad was working to help farmers develop more sustainable crops. He and his mom were alone when a terrible storm hit. The thunder was so loud the house shook. Radio announcers warned of flash floods and reported that roads and bridges were being washed out. Jacqueline and Ryan had hunkered down together, her arms wrapped around him comfortingly as she told him stories of growing up on her family's farm in the south of France.

A loud crack, worse than the thunder, startled them both, and then a giant tree limb crashed through the roof of their small house. Rain poured in as the rest of the roof was torn apart by howling winds. In moments, Ryan and his mom were drenched. Ryan was scared to death, but Jacqueline remained calm and focused. She told him they had to get across town to one of the bigger buildings and find shelter. Ryan refused—they'd get carried away in the rushing water and drown!

But his mom looked him in the eye and asked if Ryan trusted her. Of course, he told her. Then he needed to do exactly what she told him to do. She promised that she'd get them both to safety. Ryan trusted his mom more than anyone—even his dad—and she had always protected him. He finally nodded and followed her out into the violent storm. Hand in hand, they fought their way across the battered town, eventually finding refuge in a stone church.

All his life, through all the places they'd lived, the one constant Ryan could count on was his mom and dad. They had always been a team, and Ryan believed he could trust them with anything.

Now, he didn't know *what* to believe.

As he hurried down 5th Avenue, pushing his way through the throngs of people, Ryan felt confused and alone. He definitely didn't think what the agents said about his father was true. But his mom wasn't being honest with him, so he was going to have to figure out what was going on himself.

To do that, he'd need help—and he knew exactly where to find it.

Ryan arrived at the New York Public Library, passing the famous stone lions without a glance. He took the stairs two at a time to the third floor and burst into the Rose Main Reading Room. Over fifty feet high, the Rose, as it was known among students, had grand chandeliers hanging from a ceiling painted with murals of clouds. Thousands of books lined the walls, long wooden tables with brass reading lamps were filled with students. Normally, Ryan loved hanging out here—it was his favorite spot in the city for people watching—but right now, he was all business. He searched for Danny, which was no easy task considering that this one room went on for two full city blocks.

Danny told his parents that he came here to study, but what he was really interested in was the untraceable WiFi connection. Danny was a hacker, and the library was the ideal place to hone his cyber talent. With hundreds of laptops running in the Rose Room at any given time, he was virtually invisible online.

Of course, for Danny, it wasn't just the WiFi. The library also had girls. Lots of them. From all over the city. They came to study at the Rose after school.

Ryan spotted Danny across the room, whispering with two girls in private-school uniforms. They were probably fifteen, a couple of years older than Danny, but they hung on his every word. Danny just had a way.

"You'll never get those concert tickets trying to buy them through the website," Danny was telling them. "They'll sell out in seconds. But I can build a bot that'll get the best seats in the house for you."

"A bot?" one of them asked. "That's some kind of computer program, right?"

"Mine are more like works of art. I could get three tickets, we'll all go!" The girls shared a skeptical look, unsure if Danny was for real or just blowing smoke.

"Hey, you got a sec?" Ryan interrupted.

Danny was surprised to see Ryan here. "Don't tell me you blew it with Kasey already."

"I need to talk to you. Now."

Danny could tell something was up. "Think

about it," he told the girls. "You know where to find me."

As Ryan moved away, Danny caught up with him. "What's up?"

"You have your laptop, right?"

"I'm breathing, aren't I?" Danny slid into a seat at another table. He flipped open his tricked-out laptop and the screen came to life, displaying the words: THIS COMPUTER WILL SELF-DESTRUCT IN 15 SECONDS.

As the timer started counting down, Danny quickly tapped in the seventeen-digit password, his fingers moving across the keys like he was playing a piano.

"Will it really self-destruct?" Ryan asked.

Danny smiled. "Hope you never have to find out. All right, *mi amigo*, what can I do for you?"

Ryan pulled out his cell phone and opened it, showing Danny the picture he took of the man who'd followed him. "This guy was following me today. At first, I thought maybe he was CIA."

Danny rolled his eyes. "Riiight. I may be gullible, but I'm not an idiot."

"This isn't a joke—I swear."

Danny's grin faded as he realized Ryan was serious. "You're not screwing with me?"

"Not even a little bit." Danny looked back at the picture as Ryan continued. "The car he got into had diplomatic plates. So maybe not CIA, but he definitely gave off that Secret Service, spy kind of vibe. I need to find out who he is. I overheard him say my dad's name. I think my dad may be in trouble."

"What kind of trouble?"

"I don't know. Here, I snapped a picture of the plates on his car." Ryan showed him the picture of the license plate.

"You want me to hack into the Department of Motor Vehicles?"

"Can you?" Ryan knew it was a long shot, but Danny was his only chance. His mother was a member of UNESCO, the United Nations agency that dealt with cultural and educational affairs, and Danny had used her access to get into all sorts of databases and software servers around the globe.

Danny stared at his computer, brows furrowed, thinking hard. Suddenly, his face lit up with an idea. "I don't know if I can hack into the DMV, but I could probably get access to the UN's diplomatic vehicle registry. I know my mom has to fill out a form every year for her car."

"You think it'll work?"

"It's worth a try," Danny said, "but it's gonna take a while."

"Like what, a couple of days?"

Danny looked at Ryan like he'd lost his mind. "Like, a couple of *hours*. Email me all the pix."

Ryan sent the photos, then stood. "You're the best."

"Oh, I think that's already been firmly established, brother." As Ryan left, he glanced back. Danny was already deeply immersed in his search. The one thing that could distract his friend from girls was a serious hack.

CHAPTER

08

NEW YORK, USA

yan emerged from the subway station at Lexington and 63rd cautiously, searching the face of every passerby for signs of danger. The streets were now dark and quiet. Ryan worried that he was being paranoid but then remembered something his father told him before his first ice-hockey game the winter they lived in Croatia: Never second-guess your instincts. Good instincts make the difference between winning and losing. Ryan had tried to take his dad's advice but ended up getting creamed on the ice. Turns out, Croatians kick butt at hockey.

The Quinns' brownstone on 62nd Street was a prewar four-story walk-up that had been in their family for almost a hundred years. Both his grandfather and father had grown up there. Some of Ryan's favorite memories were the times spent with Granddad on his family's visits to New York. Declan Quinn told the best stories. He'd sit with Ryan in the big chairs in his study, the fire blazing and crackling, and spin tales of knights and dragons, leprechauns and windigos, the Russian witch Baba Yaga and the Japanese samurai Masashige. Stories from cultures all over the world that spoke of bravery, loyalty, and sacrifice. Ryan never forgot any of them. When Granddad died last year, it took Ryan a long time to accept that he was really gone. Living in the brownstone these past months, he thought of Granddad often.

Ryan approached the home from across the street, pausing behind a parked truck and searching the shadows. Did the man who followed him know where he lived? Not spotting anything suspicious, he headed inside. Just in case, he had his key out and ready as he ran up the steps to the front door.

Entering, he shut the door and locked the deadbolt, then started flipping on lights. Mom wasn't home yet. Perfect. Ryan wanted answers, and he knew the best chance of finding any was in the study on the bottom floor. Dumping his backpack, he hurried down the long central hallway and took the stairs down.

The entire lower floor of the brownstone had been carved out decades ago by Granddad as a large study and library. Shelves lined one entire wall, filled with an array of books on geography and history. The bottom shelf was crammed full of old maps and atlases. Ryan passed the fireplace and the two wingback chairs where he'd spent so many hours listening to his grandfather and headed to the massive desk that sat in the middle of the study.

He started opening and closing drawers, not even sure exactly what he was looking for. Paid bills, old financial statements, files on the various UN projects his father coordinated. None of it helped. As far as he could tell, everything looked totally normal.

"It's never enough. It's never enough. . . ."

Ryan jumped out of his skin at the loud noise. It took a moment for him to realize the music was the ringtone assigned to Danny on his cell phone, The Cure crooning their displeasure. Ryan snatched the phone from his pocket and answered, "Hey."

"Dude, what have you gotten yourself into?"

Danny was clearly worried.

"You found something?"

"We need to talk."

"What about the plates—"

"Not on the cell," Danny snapped. "Just stay inside and lock the doors. I'm already on the way." The connection was cut.

Ryan had never heard Danny sound so intense, and he wondered what could have him so worked up. He sat heavily in the desk chair, frustrated and anxious to have some answers.

Looking around the room, a memory drifted in at the edge of his subconscious. He was around six years old and his family had been visiting. Upstairs, Ryan had heard arguing coming from the study. Curious, he had wandered down, listening from the stairwell.

". . . It's too dangerous," his father had said.

"It's always dangerous, John. Always has been." Granddad's tone was deadly serious.

Ryan remembered a strange sound, like something metal rolling, then silence. He'd crept down the stairs and peered around the doorway.

No one had been there. His father and his grandfather: gone.

Just then, his mother had arrived upstairs, yelling out that she'd brought home his favorite ice cream. Chocolate won out over a mystery any day. He raced upstairs, forgetting all about the strange occurrence.

Sitting at the old desk now, Ryan spun around, looking at the room. Where had they gone that day? There were no doors other than the entrance from the stairs, and the only windows were up high at street level and didn't open. Ryan stood, looking at the room more closely now, analyzing everything about it. Something was bothering him, but he wasn't sure exactly what it was.

His gaze drifted up to the ceiling. The floor above this one held the living room, a dining room, and the kitchen at the far back of the brownstone. As he pictured it in his mind's eye, Ryan realized this floor and the one above weren't quite the same size. They should have been, as the brownstone was built straight up from the bottom.

Ryan moved to the exposed-brick wall at the end of the room and inspected it more closely. There were no lines in the mortar, though. Nothing to indicate that it was anything other than a normal wall. He felt stupid. What was he thinking, that there was some kind of secret entrance here? His dad was a diplomat, not Batman!

He looked down, annoyed with himself, and turned back toward the desk.

Then, he stopped.

Ryan spun back toward the wall. The mortar lines on the wall were all in perfect shape. Three bricks from the bottom, however, the mortar was cracked in strange places, almost as if it had been cut. Kneeling, he looked more closely at the bricks. Using the tips of his fingers, he grabbed the loose mortar. It pulled out with little effort and he began working more quickly. Several more pieces came out until Ryan had outlined four of the bricks, one each on top and bottom and two in the middle, making a lowercase *t* shape.

Grabbing the top brick, Ryan pulled. It came out and he looked at it in surprise; it wasn't even a full brick, only the front half of one. He set it aside, his heart beating faster, wondering what exactly he'd stumbled onto here. The other three half bricks came out just as easily, and Ryan peered into the opening he'd created.

A metal handle was nestled inside the cavity. Ryan took a step back and finally got it: The brick wall was fake. He pulled the handle. It was heavy, but the wall pivoted straight up like a garage door. Behind it was a hidden room.

CHAPTER
09

**NEW YORK,
USA**

gainst the back wall, a chest-height worktable had been carved from cedar, the smell of the old wood permeating the enclosed space. Ryan approached, passing a rack filled with equipment. He wasn't a techie, but this looked pretty sophisticated: a high-quality laser printer and scanner, a laminating machine, and a couple of other devices that he didn't recognize at all.

The worktable was covered with maps, photos, and piles of computer printouts. Ryan picked up the photos, which were grainy and taken from a long distance, like surveillance pictures. He didn't recognize anyone in them. A map of Southeast Asia was open and had been heavily marked up. The map included south-west China, Laos, and Thailand. But the focus seemed to be on the country of Andakar.

Above the table hung a giant corkboard covered with tacked-up information. Train and airline schedules were pinned beside photos of parks and what looked like old Asian temples. Ryan noticed that the train schedules were all from Andakar and looked closely at the printed captions under the temple photos. Same thing—everything here was pointing toward Andakar.

Ryan had never been there, but he knew a hard-core military government ruled Andakar with an iron fist, imprisoning, torturing, and even executing citizens who spoke out against it. Ryan had read that they recently opened their borders to tourists and were trying to promote travel in order to make money. Which seemed like a terrible idea. Who'd want to vacation in a place that treats its own people like that?

On a shelf next to the table, Ryan noticed a stack of passports from various countries—Germany, England, South Africa, Canada. Ryan flipped open the top one, his stomach sinking as he recognized his father's picture above the name Benjamin O'Hara. The others were all the same: Each one showed Dad with a different name.

Ryan glanced at the equipment on the rack, understanding its purpose now. His father had been making forged passports. Good ones, from what Ryan could tell. The next one showed a picture of his mother and another fake name. So Mom was involved, too. And there were others— a redheaded young woman and two different men Ryan didn't recognize—all with passports made out to multiple identities. Ryan's head was spinning, scrambling to process all this information.

When he opened the last one, an Irish passport, his heart nearly stopped. Looking back at him was his *own* photo and the name Thomas Dylan O'Hara. It said he lived in Dublin and that he was sixteen years old!

Ryan threw the passport down on the table and took several steps back. This couldn't be possible. The people he loved most in the world—the people he *trusted* most—what kind of secrets were they keeping from him? The CIA agents had said his father was dealing with smugglers and known criminals. Seeing the fake passports, Ryan couldn't help but wonder if it was true.

He had to find his mother. He'd make her tell him the truth, no matter how bad it was. No more lies. That was the one thing he knew: No more lies.

As he turned to leave the secret room, a scream from upstairs pierced the silence. It startled Ryan, but then instinct kicked in and he started running.

"Mom?" he yelled.

Ryan took the stairs two at a time as something crashed in the upstairs hall. His mother was in serious danger, and no matter what else was going on, Ryan would do everything possible to protect her.

Leaping up the last couple of stairs, Ryan burst around the corner to find grocery bags scattered on the ground in disarray and his mom struggling in the arms of an Asian giant, a dark-suited powerhouse of a man. In front of them stood a second man—the same Asian guy who had followed Ryan earlier!

The man held her chin with an iron grip, forcing her to look at him. "Where is Myat Kaw?"

"You'll never find out if you hurt me!" Jacqueline was scared but defiant.

Just then, the giant holding her saw Ryan at the end of the hallway. "Aung Win—the boy!"

Aung Win turned. His eyes were so dark they were almost black.

"Let her go," Ryan said, shifting instinctively into a fighting stance.

"No, Ryan—run!" The defiance was gone from Jacqueline's voice. She was kicking, thrashing, fighting like a wildcat, but the man who held her was too strong for her to break free.

Ryan charged forward, trying hard not to be completely freaked out. His father always warned that if you lose your head, you lose the fight. Dad had mostly trained in a fighting style called Krav Maga, the same street-fighting technique used by Israeli Defense Forces. It's brutal and effective—all about finding weakness and adapting to the situation, no matter how perilous or impossible it seems. And this seemed pretty impossible. Ryan had to take out at least one of the men quickly if he was going to stand a chance. He came in hard and fast with a throat strike.

But Aung Win sidestepped the blow; Ryan barely glanced his shoulder. Aung Win's retaliation was swift and fierce, a hammer blow that caught Ryan right in his solar plexus. The hit knocked the air out of Ryan. He stumbled back, gasping for air. He grabbed a side table, trying to keep his balance.

"Leave him alone. I'll tell you!" Jacqueline was desperate.

Pulling out a gun, Aung Win turned from Ryan as if he was insignificant. "I had planned to take your son. It's convenient that he has come to me." He pointed the weapon at Ryan, but his eyes never left Jacqueline's. "You will tell me where John Quinn is. You will tell me where I can find Myat Kaw. If I think you are holding anything back, I will shoot your son."

Ryan fought the panic rising in his chest. Aung Win's moves were those of a practiced killer. Ryan struggled to think of something he could do to even the odds. He glanced at the side table and saw two carved jade candlesticks his parents had bought in China.

Jacqueline looked defeated as she said, "The last time I spoke to John, he was in Thailand. He was going to cross into Andakar." Before she could continue—*Bam! Bam! Bam!*

"Dude, open up, it's me!" came from outside the front door.

The adults all turned, but Ryan took the opportunity to grab one of the candlesticks. He slammed it down on Aung Win's forearm, hearing bones crack. The gun clattered to the floor as the man gasped in pain.

"Danny," Ryan yelled, "Call the cops!"

Aung Win reacted quickly, furiously striking out at Ryan with his left hand. The blow caught Ryan on the shoulder, hitting the nerves so that his arm fell to his side like a dead weight. He staggered back, spying the gun under one of the ornate legs of their kitchen table.

In their native tongue, Aung Win barked an order to the big man, who had moved to protect Aung Win like a bodyguard. The bodyguard shoved Jacqueline forward, turned, and opened the front door.

Ryan saw Danny on the front stoop, frozen at the sight of the Goliath who towered over him. "Look out!" Ryan screamed, snapping Danny back to his senses. Danny ducked just in time, using his smaller size to evade the bodyguard's grasp, and jumped down the stairs.

In the hallway, Ryan saw Aung Win had Jacqueline by the throat. He winced, forced to use the arm Ryan had just injured to pull a plastic bag out of his pocket. Ryan dove for the gun as Aung Win ripped the bag open with his teeth and noxious fumes from the chlorophyll-soaked rag inside seeped into the air. Jacqueline jerked backward, but Aung Win held her tight with his good arm, forcing the rag over her nose and mouth.

"Let her go!" Ryan shouted, pointing the gun unsteadily at Aung Win as his mom lost consciousness. The man hefted Jacqueline in front of him as he backed toward the door.

"Go ahead and shoot," he taunted.

Ryan tried to look confident, but he'd never shot a gun before in his life. Even worse, the blow from Aung Win had left his right arm limp, and he was stuck using his bad hand. There was no way he could risk taking a shot.

"Leave us alone!" Ryan said. "Just let her go and we'll pretend this never happened." He was trying to buy time. Maybe someone heard. Maybe Danny got to make the call. Maybe someone would come to help if he could just stall them long enough. Ryan took another step forward.

"Your family should not get involved where you don't belong."

"What are you talking about? We just moved here," Ryan said. Aung Win ignored him, pulling Jacqueline out the front door and slamming it behind him. Ryan ran after them, but stumbled over the groceries that had scattered everywhere. He fell hard.

Hearing the screech of tires outside, Ryan jumped to his feet, dropping the gun so he could use his good hand to open the door. He threw it wide and saw his mother tossed into the backseat of a dark sedan. Aung Win followed right behind.

"No!" Ryan screamed, coming down the stairs. The car raced away down the street. "Stop!" But it was no use. In seconds, the car sped around the corner. Ryan watched helplessly as his mother disappeared.

CHAPTER

10

**NEW YORK,
USA**

For a few moments, Ryan stood in the empty street, frozen in shock. Only when Danny appeared at his elbow, urging him back to the sidewalk, did he notice that he was holding up traffic. Cabbies honked and swore and revved their engines, impatient to get by.

"Was that him?" Danny asked. "The guy that followed you?"

Ryan nodded, numb with fear. "They've got my mother."

"Sorry I ran—I thought that guy was gonna squash me."

"I heard them talking. They're trying to find

my dad. They think she knows where he is. She said something about him crossing over into Andakar."

"That's where it was from," Danny said. "That license plate—it's a diplomatic plate registered with Andakar's embassy."

"We need to call the police," Ryan said, turning back to the house.

"I wouldn't do that, if I were you."

Ryan and Danny both stopped short, surprised to see a young woman now standing between them and the stairs to the brownstone. With her short, severe hairstyle and alabaster skin, knee-high boots, tight pants, and leather jacket, Ryan thought she looked at least twenty. Maybe older. She seemed to have appeared out of nowhere, but then Ryan recognized her—this was the woman whose picture was on one of the forged passports in the secret room!

"If you go to the police now, both your parents are as good as dead." The woman spoke with calm assurance, but she radiated an aura of danger. Ryan wasn't sure what to make of her.

"Who are you?"

"Tasha Levi," she said, with a slight accent,

scanning the street as she spoke. "I can help your parents, but I need some information. Information that's inside your house."

"What kind of information?" Danny asked.

Tasha glanced at him, as if noticing him for the first time. "We should really have this little chat inside."

"No one is going inside or anywhere until I get some answers." Ryan was getting over his initial panic, and his tone was firm. "Who were those men?"

"I don't know."

"How do you know my parents?"

"I can't tell you that."

"Well, what are you looking for that you think you're going to find in my house?" he asked, exasperated.

"The trip your father is on, I need to know exactly where he went. I need to find out everything I can about the route he was taking."

"Why do you need to know that?" Ryan asked.

"How else am I going to find him and bring him back?" Her steady gaze was confident, and Ryan knew she was deadly serious.

"Come on," he said, pushing past her up the stairs.

Danny leaped after him, grabbing his shoulder. "What are you doing? You trust her?"

"My parents did. And right now, I've got to trust *someone*."

CHAPTER

11

**NEW YORK,
USA**

"Holy crap." Danny's eyes were huge as he looked at the secret room in the study. "What are your parents into?"

"I don't know. But I think she does." Ryan showed Tasha the passport he'd found with her photo inside. "This has your picture, but it doesn't say Tasha. It says Kathleen Connors."

Glancing at it, Tasha frowned. "I hate that name. But I do look good with red hair." She turned her attention back to the marked-up map of Andakar and all the notes, photos, and computer printouts on the worktable. She searched through everything, setting certain items aside.

"Are my parents criminals?" Ryan asked, afraid of the answer.

"Yes," she said. "In at least eight countries around the world, both John and Jacqueline Quinn would probably be put to death if they were ever caught."

Ryan felt as if he couldn't breathe, but then Tasha's expression softened, "But a criminal in one person's eyes is a hero in someone else's."

"A hero?"

"You come from a long line of them, actually. Going back over seventy years."

Ryan felt like he was on a roller coaster. "Can you please just give me a straight answer? What's going on?"

"Have you ever heard of Varian Fry?" Tasha continued her search as she spoke.

Ryan exchanged a glance with Danny, both of them shaking their heads. "Who was he?" Ryan asked.

"In the beginning, nobody. An American journalist who was a foreign correspondent in Europe during the 1930s. But as the Nazis came to power in Germany, Varian Fry saw firsthand how the Jewish people were being treated. It sickened him, and it made him want to do something. To help in whatever way he could."

"What does that have to do with Ryan's parents?" Danny asked. "They weren't born yet."

"Shut up and you'll find out." Tasha gave him a withering look.

"Wow," Danny said. "Harsh."

"Over the next several years," Tasha continued, "things in Europe went from bad to worse as World War II erupted and Adolf Hitler's power grew. By 1940, the Germans had occupied France and anyone of Jewish descent was in danger of being sent to a concentration camp."

As she told the tale, Tasha's impatience faded. This was not merely history she was repeating, Ryan understood, but something deeply personal to her.

"As a foreign correspondent, Varian Fry was allowed to visit France after the occupation. On the surface, he appeared to be just another American reporter writing about the war. Secretly, though, he was working with a group of people who felt the same way he did. A group of regular people like himself who refused to sit back and do nothing while atrocities occurred all around them. They called themselves the Emergency Rescue Committee."

Ryan looked back to the hidden room, to the map and all the information, starting to figure out where this might be heading. He looked back to Tasha. "My great-grandfather, I think he was in France during World War II."

Tasha nodded. "He was. In fact, he was one of the first members of the Emergency Rescue Committee. It was formed here in New York, with the mission to save as many of the refugees as possible. Everyone knew that Hitler was intent on killing every anti-Nazi intellectual, artist, and writer he could get his hands on. People like Marc Chagall, Marcel Duchamp, Max Ernst. All trapped in France, knowing they could be dragged off at any moment, never to be seen again. The committee's goal was to help them escape."

"Like an underground railroad," Ryan said.

"Exactly. Over the next year and a half, Varian Fry, your great-grandfather, and a network of allies managed to smuggle over two thousand people out of France to freedom in the United States. It was the most successful operation of its kind during the war."

Ryan wanted to believe what she was telling him, but certain things still didn't make sense. "But why wouldn't they tell me that my great-grandfather was some kind of hero? I never heard anything about that."

"Yeah," Danny said, "and what does any of

that have to do with *Andakar*?"

Tasha rummaged through the drawers of the worktable as she continued. "Eventually, politics and infighting brought about the end of the group. The last thing the American government wanted was a bunch of rebels off fighting their own secret war. Fry was forced to return to the United States and, publicly at least, the Emergency Rescue Committee was disbanded."

Tasha leaned down and pulled open a drawer beneath the table, revealing rows of files, some of them quite old. She pulled a handful of files out as she spoke. "But your great-grandfather and a few others refused to let it go. If they couldn't rescue people with the support of the American government, then they'd do it on their own. The Emergency Rescue Committee lived on—even if it had to exist in secret."

She shoved the files into Ryan's arms. "For over seventy years, your family has been part of a network that helps people escape from some of the most dangerous places in the world."

She went back to the worktable as Ryan looked at the names on the files he held. *Tibet— Cuba—North Korea—Sri Lanka*. Each one held information and photos on another person rescued from imprisonment or death. Putting the pieces together now, Ryan realized that his father's job as a diplomat had been the perfect cover, allowing him to go from country to country without being suspected. Until now. Now, something had gone wrong. He looked up, remembering what Aung Win had asked his mother.

"Who is Myat Kaw?" he asked.

"With any luck," Tasha said, picking up the fake Kathleen Connors passport, "Myat Kaw is the person that's going to lead me to your father."

CHAPTER

12

**NEW YORK,
USA**

ait!" Ryan had to hurry along the sidewalk to keep up with Tasha's quick pace. "What about my mom? We have to find her."

"Where would you even start looking?" Tasha carried the map and printouts in a file under her arm. She had spent fewer than ten minutes booking flights and making calls before leaving the study, with Ryan right on her heels. "Your mother could be anywhere. The best chance we have of getting her back is finding your father."

"Then I'll go with you."

"No way. I can't help them if I have to babysit you." Tasha lifted her leg over the seat of a slick, black Kawasaki motorcycle parked at the curb.

Grabbing her helmet from behind, she gave Ryan a sympathetic look. "Go stay with your friend there for a few days. And don't come back to the house—it's not safe anymore. I'll be in touch."

Before he could argue, she hit the ignition switch with her right thumb and the motorcycle roared to life.

"But how do I get in touch with you?" Ryan asked over the noise.

"You don't. Just keep out of sight until this is over."

"Tasha—" Ryan started, but she was already racing down the street and into the night.

Ryan was sick of people disappearing on him, and Tasha was nuts if she thought he was just gonna sit tight and do nothing. He sprinted back to the brownstone, fueled by anger and frustration. He had to find some way to help his parents.

By the time he got back downstairs to the study, Danny was already typing at a furious pace on Ryan's father's computer. "Andakar's main embassy is in Washington, DC, but I'm accessing New York property records. If the embassy owns a place in the city, that might be where they took your mom."

"Good," Ryan said, moving past him to the secret room.

"So your parents are, like, insanely awesome."

"My parents are liars." Ryan jerked open drawers, searching through the remaining files.

Danny spun around in the desk chair. "They would have told you, eventually."

"They should have told me a long time ago."

"Look at all that's happened. It's dangerous. They were just trying to protect you."

"Well, that didn't work out so well, did it?" Ryan couldn't help the anger he felt and, in a way, he actually needed it. Fear would stop him cold, but anger kept him moving.

Ryan found a folder filled with credit cards, all made out to the identities on the various passports. He flipped through them, finding that one of the credit cards was made out to Thomas O'Hara, the name on his own fake passport.

Ryan's cell phone vibrated in his pocket and he snatched it out, praying it was his mother. But when he read "Blocked" on the Caller ID screen, an ominous feeling gripped him.

"Hello?"

"Ryan! Don't listen—"

"Mom?!" Her cries tore right to his heart. He wanted to leap through the phone somehow and save her. But all he could do was helplessly hold the phone in his clenched hands. "Mom, I'll find you!"

"I want to speak to John Quinn. Now—or you will never see your mother again." Ryan recognized Aung Win's voice and tried to calm down.

"He's not here. I don't know where he is."

"Then your mother dies. I want Myat Kaw!"

"Don't hurt her. I swear I don't know this Myat Kaw or where my dad is or *anything*."

There was a moment of silence, and Ryan feared Aung Win had hung up. "Fine. Tell John Quinn I will trade your mother for Myat Kaw."

"Aren't you listening—I don't know where he is!"

"I'm sure you have some way to contact him. Tell John Quinn he has five days. If I do not have Myat Kaw by Saturday, your mother dies. And if I even suspect you've spoken to the police or anyone else about this, I will kill her immediately. Five days."

"How am I supposed to find—"

But the call was already disconnected.

"Oh my god," Danny muttered. "We have to tell the cops."

"He said he'll kill her. And he's a total psycho—he'll do it."

"What choice do we have? Your dad's missing, that motorcycle girl took off—we have to do *something*."

Ryan didn't know what to do. Maybe Danny was right. Calling the police made the most sense. But what if his mom died because he did what Aung Win told him not to, and it was all his fault?

"Tasha said the best way to help Mom was to find Dad . . ." Abruptly, he stopped, a thought popping into his head. In three long strides he was at the worktable, picking up the fake passport with his picture.

"O'Hara . . ." he mumbled, wheels spinning. Ryan had an idea—a crazy idea, but it might be his only chance to save his mom.

CHAPTER
13

**NEW YORK,
USA**

"Flight two-eight-one, China Star service to Taiwan, is now boarding. All passengers please report to gate five."

Ryan dodged in and out of the crowd at JFK Airport. He was cutting it close after getting caught in the long security line. If he missed this flight, he knew he might never make it to Andakar. He gripped the plane ticket and the fake passport tightly, his backpack bumping as he ran.

Without Danny's help, he never would have made it this far. Danny had been able to track back through the history on his father's computer and find information on the plane ticket that Tasha had purchased. Using the credit card with the Thomas O'Hara name, Ryan had booked a seat for himself on the same flight out.

Ryan finally made it to the boarding area for gate five, scanning the line of impatient passengers. There! Near the front, he saw a woman with brilliant red hair. Ryan pushed his way through the passengers, hurrying to reach her before she handed over her ticket and disappeared into the plane.

"Hey, cuz, wait up!" Ryan called.

The redhead swiveled around and Tasha stared at him in disbelief. To her credit, she never broke character, but Ryan could see the daggers in her eyes.

"Hey . . . *cuz*," Tasha said, as the agent taking tickets glanced between them.

Ryan handed his ticket to the agent. "I thought you were gonna wait to get in line until I got back from the bathroom?"

Tasha looked ready to throttle him but played along. "No. I think you completely *misunderstood* what I told you."

"Oh, I understood," Ryan said. "But when a guy's gotta go, he's gotta go."

The gate agent handed Ryan's ticket back. "You're not seated together. Maybe you can ask one of the other passengers to change with you."

"We'll do that. Thanks." Ryan and Tasha moved into the gangway leading to the plane.

The moment they were out of earshot, Tasha whispered fiercely, "You can't come with me."

"They're my family."

"You'll only slow me down," she hissed.

"I can help."

"How? You're just a kid!" They were nearing the plane, and Tasha knew she was running out of options.

"I don't know how—yet," Ryan admitted. "But you're crazy if you think I'm sitting around here and doing nothing." Ryan stepped across the threshold and onto the plane. "I'm going to Andakar."

PART TWO

INTO THE LION'S DEN

CHAPTER

14

**OPEN SKIES,
ANDAKAR**

Ryan executed a Hindu Shuffle and a One-Handed Triple Cut, then worked on his Double Lifts for a while. He always kept a deck of cards with him to practice these sleight-of-hand skills, the most important element in most magic tricks. Though he'd been practicing for years, his growing hands were finally big enough for him to manipulate the cards more easily. He didn't even have to concentrate on the movements anymore, making it almost like a form of meditation. The cards helped him think, which was about all he'd been doing for the last twenty hours as he and Tasha flew halfway around the world.

How could he not have known his mom and

dad were living this secret life? It didn't seem possible. Through all the different towns and countries, the one constant he could always rely on was his parents. They were his rock.

But now he was questioning everything.

Was this stupid Emergency Rescue Committee the reason he had been forced to move all the time? Was it why he never had a regular life or got to stay in one place long enough to make real friends? Why were all those people whose names he saw in the ERC files more important to his parents than their own family? Because obviously, being part of this underground group was dangerous. Ryan's dad was missing and his mom had been kidnapped—it didn't get more dangerous than that!

All Ryan wanted was a normal teenager's life. To hang with friends, hear all the ridiculous drama and gossip, maybe play baseball on a real American team. He was finally living the life he'd dreamed of. For the first time, Ryan was starting to feel like a regular kid. He should be doing homework or grabbing a slice of pizza with Danny.

Instead, he was on a plane flying around the globe again.

"Your father furrows his brow just like you do

when he's angry." Tasha studied Ryan from the seat next to him.

"I'm not angry," he said, packing his playing cards back into their case.

Tasha looked away again. "Whatever."

Ryan still didn't know what to make of this mysterious young woman. For the entire first flight, from New York to Taiwan, she had mostly slept, barely acknowledging his presence. He had a million questions, but she pretty much blew him off, still mad that he had come along. Now, their second flight was about to end and they'd be in Andakar. Ryan wanted some answers.

"How come I've never met you?" he asked. "I know most of my parents' friends."

"Members of the committee have as little outside contact with each other as possible."

Ryan was surprised to finally get an actual response. "Did you do these rescues with my parents?"

"Occasionally. That's how the ERC works, a network of people around the globe, each just a stop along the way. Only a few people know who all the members are. It's safer that way."

"Then how do you contact each other? Because maybe we could get other people to help us. Maybe someone knows where we can find my dad."

"That's not how it works, kid."

"We need all the help we can get. How are we supposed to find one man in a whole country of people?"

"I'll find him. It's what I do." Tasha leaned her head back, closing her eyes as if the conversation was over.

Before Ryan could protest, the flight attendant broke in with an announcement, which she repeated in several languages: "Ladies and gentlemen, we will be landing shortly at Panai International Airport. As we start our descent, please make sure your seat backs and tray tables are in their full upright positions. Welcome to Andakar."

Ryan turned to the window, taking in the harsh and unforgiving landscape passing beneath them. Dense forests of towering trees covered rocky hillsides. This close to the city, there was still no sign of civilization. As the plane cleared the hills, Ryan spotted a lone pagoda perched precariously halfway down a steep slope, the sun glinting off its dome. It was massive, but looked impossible to reach, isolated by the wilderness around it.

"Wow," Ryan said, craning his neck to get a better glimpse.

Tasha glanced past him through the window. "Andakar is a land of contrasts. Ancient, yet wracked with modern problems. Primitive, but starkly beautiful. It's also one of the most perilous countries in the world. There are eyes and ears everywhere, and the secret police won't hesitate to lock you up."

"I thought they were trying to attract tourists. Throwing people in jail doesn't sound like the kind of thing you put in a travel brochure."

"The military regime only opened up the borders because they want Western countries to invest in their economy. Tourists see only what the government wants them to see: remarkable temples, colorful parades, exotic jungles. The ruling class in Andakar gets richer every day while the people starve."

"And this Myat Kaw, what did he do to make them so mad?"

"Exposed them for the liars they are. Myat Kaw's been blogging about Andakar for over a year now, revealing secrets about the military regime. No one knows Myat Kaw's identity, but judging from the information he's released, it seems likely that he's high up in the military. He has access to details that only someone on the inside would know."

"And my dad went there to rescue him?"

Tasha looked unsure. "From what I read in his files, I think Quinn was planning to sneak Myat Kaw out of the country and across the border to safety."

"Then he must have known who Myat Kaw was. How else could he help him escape?"

"If he did, he didn't leave any record of it at your house. Which isn't a surprise. Quinn has always been insistent on keeping information secret. He believes it's safer for everyone that way." Tasha's frustration was clear. "Your father can be quite irritating."

"How do you know Dad didn't get Myat Kaw out already? Maybe they're just hiding somewhere until things blow over."

"I don't think so," she said. "Quinn's never off the grid for this long. Something went wrong."

Ryan was quiet a moment, then asked what had been in his mind the whole time. "Do you think he's already dead?"

"I certainly hope not." Tasha didn't even try to be comforting.

Ryan looked out the window once more. Up ahead, the outskirts of the city appeared. The rugged terrain of the hills gave way to urban sprawl. Factories belching smoke were sur-rounded by older apartment buildings that spread out in all directions. Even from up here, the disorder and poverty were evident.

As the plane landed, Ryan couldn't shake the question that kept plaguing him: Why was his father willing to risk his life to save some guy he didn't even know?

CHAPTER
15

**PANAI,
ANDAKAR**

The moment he got off the plane and took his first steps into Andakar, Ryan could sense how different things were there. It was weirdly quiet, a kind of hush in the terminal where all the passengers disembarked. The airport itself had an aura of faded glamour, as if it had once been impressive but had been neglected for far too long. The smell of mold, like in the boy's locker room at school, hung in the air.

There were only a handful of tourists and they were generally older. Ryan and Tasha were by far the youngest people arriving.

"Remember, we're cousins, Thomas O'Hara and Kathleen Connors, traveling from Ireland—"

"I *got* it," Ryan shot back, annoyed. They'd been over the cover story multiple times. But being a chameleon is what Ryan had done most of his life, and he was good at it. Faking an accent, changing his body language to fit the situation—that was easy for him. Of course, he'd never traveled under an assumed identity. He took a deep breath, calming his nerves.

Ryan followed the line of passengers toward passport control. As they entered the security area, soldiers in pale gray uniforms stood on each side of the passage, watching everyone with undisguised suspicion. The soldiers wore black tactical vests over their uniforms and carried submachine guns. But Ryan was used to tight security at a lot of the places they had traveled, so he wasn't intimidated.

One of the soldiers shifted his gaze to Ryan, who was caught by surprise. Ryan looked away a moment too late. The soldier's full attention was now on him, eyeing the backpack Ryan wore slung over his shoulder. As he followed Tasha through the doorway, Ryan's path was suddenly blocked by the soldier's submachine gun.

The man barked at him in his native language, which Ryan now recognized as Andalese, the same language he had heard on the plane and from Aung Win back in New York. Ryan adopted what he hoped was a confused, naive expression. Reminding himself he was supposed to be Irish, he said, "Sure lookit, I'm just visiting. What's the problem then?" A few steps ahead, Tasha stopped and turned back.

The soldier spoke again in his language, and Ryan smiled sheepishly. "Sorry—you speak English?"

"Parent?" the soldier asked. "Where is parent?"

Tasha responded before Ryan could. "I'm his cousin. We're traveling together." Tasha's own voice lilted with a perfect Irish accent.

The soldier looked between them, then motioned Ryan away from the others. "This way," he said. Tasha took a step to follow, but another soldier stopped her.

"Not you," the second soldier ordered. "You, there." Ryan could see Tasha struggling with what to do, not wanting to lose Ryan, but not having any good options.

"It's okay, cuz," he told her with more confidence than he felt. "I'll see you in a few minutes." Ryan walked in front of the soldier who guided him away. As they arrived at the security checkpoint, the soldier began speaking to a uniformed immigration official and pointing at Ryan.

Ryan had been going through security checkpoints all his life. There were usually long lines and waiting always felt like forever. His parents would play games with him to help pass the time. One of his favorites was "I've Got a Secret." His dad would whisper outrageous "secrets" to him, usually something that made him laugh, like the man checking passports was nicknamed Mr. Fart-a-Lot. They'd joke about it while they waited, but once it was their turn to hand over their passports, the goal of the game was to keep a straight face and never let on.

Ryan wasn't too good at it in the beginning, and there were plenty of officials around the world who probably thought he was a little nuts as he laughed hysterically for no apparent reason. But over the years, he got better, until he could keep a straight face no matter how hysterical the secret was.

"You are visiting Andakar on your own?" The immigration official spoke perfect English with a slight British accent, holding out his hand for Ryan's passport.

Ryan handed it over with a smile. "I'm with my cousin. She's my legal guardian. This guy wouldn't let her come with me."

"Someone else will speak with your cousin. Thomas O'Hara," he read, examining the passport carefully.

"Tommy," Ryan said. "That's what my friends call me."

The official looked up at him with a cold, fake smile. "And what is the reason for your visit?"

"To see this incredible country—they say it's bang on! We're gonna go down to the beaches, and then, hopefully, get to do one of those zipline tours through the jungle. You ever done that? The lads say it's deadly cool." Ryan told himself to tone it down a bit, he was sounding a little *too* Irish.

The official appraised him, then reached out a hand for his backpack. "You have no drugs?"

Drugs? Is that what this was about? "Absolutely not," Ryan said. "I'd never do drugs." That was one thing Ryan *didn't* have to lie about.

The official looked through the bag, which contained mostly clothes, toiletries, a stash of chocolate, and a couple of baseball caps. "We have difficulties with young people believing they can come here and . . . party? That is the word, yes?"

"I'm just here to see your beautiful country,"

Ryan said with complete conviction. The immigration official nodded, handing Ryan his backpack. With one efficient movement, he stamped the passport, then held it out.

"Enjoy your stay."

"Thanks. I plan to." Ryan took his passport and hurried away, trying to keep the grin off his face. Across the hall, he saw with relief that Tasha's passport was also getting stamped. They'd done it.

But even more important, Ryan had made a discovery that he was just beginning to understand. The games he'd grown up playing with his parents, like "Follow-the-Monkey" and "I've Got a Secret," weren't just for fun. They were training exercises. Ryan's parents had been secretly preparing him for this kind of assignment his entire life.

CHAPTER
16

**PANAI,
ANDAKAR**

Ryan had been right about the city—
the streets of Panai were chaotic. The
sidewalks were crammed with people
pushing past one another, knocking into Ryan
without a second thought as he tried to keep up
with Tasha. A decrepit old bus spewed a cloud of
exhaust right into his face as it pulled away from
the curb. Ryan hacked and coughed, wishing he
could stop at one of the countless vendors that
lined the sidewalk and grab a drink. But Tasha
never looked back, and he wasn't about to risk
losing her.

Ryan had traveled throughout Asia and his
family had even lived in Bangkok for six months,
but he had never seen such a vibrant display of

color as here in Panai. Though the roads were dirty and most of the buildings in disrepair, everywhere Ryan looked there was purple, pink, orange, or yellow. It was as if the locals refused to allow the reality of their daily lives to define their world. The only thing detracting from the festive atmosphere was the presence of gray-uniformed soldiers with machine guns on every corner.

"We have to hurry," Tasha said.

Ryan ran to catch up as she navigated through the crowd. "Where are we going?"

"Across town. We'll stay with a friend tonight, then start out first thing in the morning."

"Who's this friend? Do they know where my dad is?"

Tasha never stopped scanning the faces around them as she answered. "Friends are people who help out the ERC. They provide places to stay, transportation, sometimes just information or access. They put themselves at risk every time they open their doors to us."

Ryan and Tasha arrived at a large, open plaza teeming with people. An ornately carved pagoda occupied the center of the busy square. The pagoda's roof, a carved dome that tapered to a long, thin spire, was almost four stories high and covered in gold leaf.

"Take my picture," Tasha said. Ryan was confused by her goofy grin as she took a few steps backward so he could get a better shot. They didn't have time for sightseeing! But Tasha was insistent, "Take my picture, *Tommy*."

Ryan pulled out his phone, switching it to camera. As he raised it to snap a few pix, Tasha's bizarre actions became clear. While he shot pictures, she was looking *behind* him, searching the crowd. Ryan realized he still had a lot to learn.

Tasha came close and whispered, "Cross the plaza to the opposite side, then keep going straight down the street on the other side. Be natural, not obvious. Take your time. You're a *tourist*." She started to walk away.

"Where are you going?"

"I want to make sure we're clear before we travel to the safe house." Before Ryan could protest, Tasha was gone, disappearing like a ghost into the crowd. His instinct was to look for anyone following them, but he stopped, reminding himself to be natural. He was a tourist.

Ryan made his way across the plaza, focusing on the pagoda. It was pretty awesome, covered in intricate carvings and surrounded on all sides by hundreds of small sculptures of the

Buddha. He stopped in front of a sign, reading that the Ashoka Temple was over two thousand years old.

As he passed the entrance, Ryan noticed an old monk, bald and wrapped in a blood-red robe, watching him. The monk smiled and bowed slightly. With a nod of his head, Ryan returned the bow and was surprised when the monk stepped forward. The man took Ryan's hand and gently slipped a string bracelet around his wrist. It was simple but beautiful, with interwoven strands of red and yellow.

"Tasmati ca niva," the monk said, bowing once more. Ryan had no idea what he was saying.

"It is a blessing," said a passing woman, noticing Ryan's uncertainty. "Very good luck. You say, '*Tin ba dai.*'"

Ryan turned back to the monk, making another small bow, the bracelet firmly in place. *"Tin ba dai,"* he repeated, then faced the helpful woman. "Thank you."

But she was looking beyond him now, her expression darkening. She nodded curtly and abruptly walked away. Ryan turned to see what had spooked her: One of the soldiers was staring right at him with suspicion. Ryan gave what he hoped was an innocent smile, and then started across the plaza once more.

Making it to the other side, he crossed the street, as Tasha had instructed. He kept walking, unsure how far he should go. What if they really were being followed? If something had happened to Tasha, he had no idea where he was supposed to go or what he should do. Only now, standing by himself in the middle of this busy foreign city did Ryan realize how alone he'd be if he lost Tasha. He didn't know anybody here, didn't know the language, and had no idea how he'd ever find Dad on his own. And if he didn't find his dad, how could he hope to help his mom? He felt his stomach twisting, panic threatening as the minutes dragged by.

Where *was* she?

The screech of tires startled Ryan and he whirled around. An old Peugeot hatchback that had seen better days stopped at the curb, the passenger door swinging open and nearly hitting him.

"Get in," Tasha commanded from the driver's side.

Ryan didn't hesitate, jumping in and slamming

the door closed. The car's engine made a grinding noise as Tasha shifted into gear and sped off.

"Where'd you get this?" Ryan asked.

"Stole it," Tasha said matter-of-factly. Ryan stared at her—was she being serious? Seeing his expression, she rolled her eyes. "Don't worry, we'll give it back. Eventually."

Ryan leaned back against the seat. "So we're thieves now."

Tasha grinned. "You're just like your father." The way she said it, Ryan knew it wasn't meant as a compliment.

CHAPTER 17

**PANAI,
ANDAKAR**

Darkness had fallen by the time the Peugeot rattled to a stop on one of Panai's countless winding roads. This neighborhood was more residential, the streets lined with apartment buildings, most of which were falling apart. Telephone cables and power lines snaked through the air, and the sounds of families eating and laughing wafted from open windows.

"We have to hurry," Tasha said, getting out of the car. "The show starts in less than five minutes."

"What show?" Ryan grabbed his backpack, following as she moved quickly down the street.

"You'll see." Ryan was almost getting used

to the way Tasha seldom answered a question directly. He didn't even bother asking anything further because he had the feeling she kind of enjoyed tormenting him.

They made it to the end of the block. Tasha paused, confirming once more that they were in the clear, before she turned the corner onto a busier street. A few storefronts away, a small crowd of adults and children were gathered on the sidewalk. As Tasha and Ryan approached, the group began filing inside what Ryan could now see was a theater. The marquee was in a language Ryan couldn't read, but it was translated into English at the bottom: "Mama Nan's Marionette Theater!"

"Puppets?"

Tasha didn't even bother to respond, mixing in with the patrons as they drifted inside. Ryan followed, falling into step beside two chattering younger kids.

The theater wasn't very big, but was surprisingly nice, with red velvet seats for the audience and heavy curtains on all sides. Down front, the proscenium surrounding the stage was decorated to look like an imperial palace. Almost as soon as Ryan and Tasha took their seats, the lights dimmed and the curtain rose.

A gong struck three times, then a burst of music erupted, a strange melody of ill-timed drumbeats and tinkling bells. Against a mountain landscape backdrop, two marionettes appeared, their strings rising above their heads to where the unseen puppet masters controlled them. The puppets were tall and elaborately decorated. One appeared to be a demon of some kind, with emerald-green skin, red-jeweled eyes, and fangs like a vampire; the other was a young princess with silk robes that twirled when she spun around.

Ryan was so transfixed by the show that he jerked in shock when a hand grabbed his shoulder. He spun around to find a young man right behind their seats. The man put a finger to his lips and motioned for them to follow. Tasha got up immediately and slipped out. Ryan cast one sidelong glance back at the show, then joined them.

Moving through the shadows, they followed the young man behind the stage. All around, lifeless marionettes hung from the ceiling, seeming to stare at Ryan as he passed. Backstage, the magic was gone. These puppets gave Ryan the creeps.

They arrived at a rickety wooden stairway

and the young man motioned for them to go up alone. He disappeared into the shadows and Ryan followed Tasha up the steep stairway. At the top was a single door that she entered without hesitating. As Ryan came in, Tasha closed the door behind him.

"What do we do now?" The distraction of the theater already fading, Ryan was anxious to get started. The flight to Andakar had taken almost a full day, and he couldn't stop worrying about his parents.

"Now," Tasha said, "we sleep."

"What? I don't want to sleep—I want to find my dad."

Tasha tossed down her bag. "My contact in Panai says it's not safe for him to meet until ten tomorrow morning. And you barely slept on the plane. In the ERC, one of the first things you learn is to sleep when you can. You may not get another chance for a long time." Tasha looked over the room, which had a small sink in the corner and a large worktable filled with string, wood, and paint for making marionettes. "Not bad for a crash pad."

Ryan watched in disbelief as Tasha bunched up some fabric to create a makeshift pillow, then settled down to sleep. She glanced up at him. "Seriously. There's nothing we can do right now." She turned over to face the wall, ending the conversation.

Ryan crossed the room and sat, discouraged and angry. He'd brought a stash of chocolate and grabbed a small square from his backpack. Unfortunately, it did nothing to help his anxiety. He pulled a photograph from his pocket, unfolding it to see his mom and dad smiling back at him. It was a family picture taken on one of their countless camping expeditions. Though he was still upset by the secrets they'd been keeping, all he cared about was getting his parents back home. The fear that he might never see either of them again was overwhelming.

After a few minutes, Ryan was surprised to hear steady breathing coming from Tasha. She really did know how to grab sleep when she could!

But Ryan couldn't just do nothing. Time was of the essence. Folding the picture and returning it to his pocket, he looked back to the window. Outside, a fire escape led to the roof. He quietly pulled out his cell phone and powered it on. Because of all his traveling, Ryan had a phone that could work pretty much anywhere in the world as long as it had a signal.

Ryan crept over and raised the window carefully. With one last glance at Tasha, he stepped out onto the fire escape.

CHAPTER
18

**PANAI,
ANDAKAR**

From the roof, Ryan could see Panai extending in all directions. For a city this large, there was surprisingly little light, not at all like the near-constant brightness of New York. The phone beeped as it finished powering up and connected to the local service carrier. Ryan was excited to discover he had two voice mails. He hit the play button, praying one of them was from his dad.

But the first was Danny, telling Ryan he had some new information and to call no matter what time it was. He hit play on the second message.

"Ryan, it's Mom. I'm okay . . ."

Hearing his mother's voice, Ryan was flooded

with relief. She was still alive! He hadn't even realized how scared he was that it might already be too late to save her. At least now he knew he had a chance. But his hope was dashed as the message continued.

"I've told these men we don't know about any of this—"

Aung Win's gruff voice barked through the speaker. "Four days. You will produce Myat Kaw or you will never hear Jacqueline Quinn's voice again."

"Let go!" Jacqueline's tone was indignant, but then the message abruptly cut off.

Ryan stared at the phone a moment. He felt so powerless. But he knew sitting up here agonizing about his mom's situation wouldn't help her—he needed to *do* something. He dialed Danny's number. Whatever information he'd found might be useful. The time difference between here and New York was twelve hours, so Danny would be in school now. The phone rang three times, and Ryan worried that Danny wouldn't answer.

"Ohmygod, dude, you're still alive!" Danny's hushed voice over the line made Ryan instantly feel a little better.

"Yeah, we made it to Andakar. But we still

don't know where my dad is."

"Hold on," Danny whispered. Ryan could hear shuffling and realized Danny was hiding his phone. "Miss Ellison, so sorry—kind of a crisis—can I run to the bathroom?" Ryan couldn't hear Miss Ellison's response, but he assumed it wasn't positive because Danny suddenly wailed, "Ooooo! Total emergency! Maybe both ends!" That must've done the trick because he could hear Danny moving now. "Thanks, Miss Ellison!"

Moments later, Danny had made it out of the classroom. "You owe me," he told Ryan. "I'm gonna be living that down for years."

"Did you find anything?"

"Maybe. I took your dad's computer with me and spent last night digging through it. He had some pretty impressive encryption."

"But you got in?"

"It took a while, but yeah. I got a little obsessed. Deep down in one of the root directories, I found a whole group of deleted emails from right before your dad left."

"How'd you find them if they were deleted?" Ryan asked.

"Delete doesn't really get rid of anything from your computer. It just hides it. If you know where to look, you can find it again. The thing is, it's gonna take me a while to put the emails into a shape where we can read them. Right now, it's like they went through a paper shredder—all little bits of data that have to be put back together."

Ryan was disappointed. "So they're no real help?"

"Slow down, Dr. Downer, I'm not done yet. I was able to find an IP address in the email headers. The IP address tells you where the emails were sent from."

"This is the good news part, right?"

Danny didn't hide his excitement. "All the emails came from Panai!"

"Myat Kaw," Ryan said, getting a first tingling of hope. "It had to be Myat Kaw and my dad arranging the rescue."

"That's what I figured, too. The problem is, I can't get a physical address from an IP number. I've got my desktop at home running a program to patch the emails back together, but so far the only helpful thing I dug up was the name Kali Thawar. It came up a few times in the last couple of emails."

Ryan started back toward the fire escape. "I'll ask Tasha. Maybe she knows what it is."

"*Hello?* Did I *say* I was finished?" Danny

chided. "I did some research and found out that the Kali Thawar is this hotel that was built there by the British back in the early 1900s. Google says it closed down years ago but doesn't say what it is today. It's about a mile from where you are right now."

"You know where I am?"

"I'm looking at your location on that cell tracker app I created. It uses your phone's GPS—but I can only see you if your cell's on. I'm texting you the address now."

Ryan finally had something he could use. "Okay, I'm gonna check it out. Thanks. I'll have to turn off the phone to save the battery, but I'll call you if anything comes up." Ryan ended the call and stepped back onto the fire escape stairs.

For a moment, he considered waking up Tasha and telling her about the old hotel. But she'd just want to wait until morning. This was Ryan's first real lead to find his dad, and he wasn't willing to waste another second.

Ryan hurried down the fire escape, dropping the last few feet to the ground. He raced off through the murky alleys of Panai.

CHAPTER
19

**PANAI,
ANDAKAR**

*T*he Kali Thawar had obviously started out as a grand and luxurious hotel. Standing three stories high and occupying an entire block, it was a massive building. Even now, after years of neglect, Ryan could see how impressive it must have been in its day, with a sweeping entrance, huge bay windows, and elegant columns. But it sure wasn't a hotel now.

Instead of bellboys greeting guests, the Kali Thawar had soldiers with machine guns slung over their shoulders keeping everyone out. The gates were closed, and barbed wire adorned the top of the metal fence that surrounded the property.

Staying in the shadows, Ryan circled the

building, trying to figure out its purpose. He spotted a few soldiers roaming the grounds and two more at a smaller back gate, which looked like it was probably used for deliveries. All these soldiers wore the same dark-blue uniforms, different from the drab gray of the men at the airport and in the city. None appeared particularly alert. This seemed to be their regular routine.

The guards and heavy security convinced Ryan his father must be a prisoner here. That would explain why they hadn't heard from him. Dad and Myat Kaw had discussed the Kali Thawar right before he disappeared. Ryan had to get inside and find his dad. But how was he going to get past the security patrols? The metal fencing and barbed wire surrounded the compound on all sides.

Every fifty feet or so, palm trees had been planted that rose higher than the hotel itself. They were thin and regal, creating a stately appearance. Looking at them, Ryan was struck by an inspiration: Those trees could be his way onto the grounds.

When he was nine, Ryan's family had lived for several months in Belize, a country in the Caribbean with gorgeous beaches, incredible snorkeling, and thousands of palm trees. Ryan got to know the local kids and they laughed at him when they learned he couldn't climb a palm tree; they'd all been doing it their whole lives. It took a lot of painful falls and scraped skin on the soles of his feet, but Ryan was soon able to climb the tallest palms with the best of them. He even learned to carry a machete on his back so he could hack off coconuts.

The only way he knew to climb a palm tree was barefoot, so Ryan unlaced his high-tops. Stuffing his socks in his pocket, he tied the laces of the shoes together and wrapped them loosely around his neck. He waited in the shadows until the roaming sentries passed, knowing he had to time this perfectly, then darted across the street.

The secret to climbing a palm is knowing how to apply pressure in the right directions. With his back to the metal fence, Ryan wrapped his arms around the thin trunk. At the same time, he placed his bare feet, one on top of the other, in front of him on the tree. By *pushing* with his feet while *pulling* with his hands, Ryan maintained a constant balance of pressure that kept his body in place. After every step, he raised his arms a little higher. Once you got the motion down, it was easy—the kids of Belize could scale the highest palm trees in seconds.

And that's exactly what Ryan did, the movements coming back to him instinctually even though he hadn't climbed in a few years. He could feel the tough bark scraping the soft skin on the bottom of his feet, but he didn't stop. When he was up far enough, Ryan looked behind him. He was a couple of feet higher than the barbed wire, which meant this was at least a ten-foot jump to the ground. If he missed, he'd be cut to pieces, and would probably get arrested and thrown in jail.

Before he could talk himself out of it, Ryan counted down—three, two, one!—and pushed out with his legs as hard as he could. Ryan soared over the fence and the razor-sharp wire, hanging in the air for what seemed like forever. He landed on the ground with a hard crunch. Ryan rolled with the impact, throwing himself into a somersault that knocked the breath out of him.

Gasping for air, Ryan turned over, shocked and surprised to discover he hadn't twisted an ankle or broken any bones. He knew he couldn't stay out in the open like this. He forced himself to get up and move. Keeping low, he ran to the side of the hotel, gravel stinging the soles of his feet like needle pricks, making it hard to move fast. He hid behind the shrubbery that lined the walls, listening hard for any indication that he had been spotted. After a moment to catch his breath, Ryan put his socks and shoes back on and scanned the area. The coast was clear.

Creeping around to the back, Ryan spotted an entrance that had apparently been used by the hotel's staff. There was no one around, so he cautiously moved to the door and peered through the glass panes. The door opened onto a back hallway that was empty. He tried the handle. It was unlocked.

With a deep breath and a quick, quiet prayer, Ryan slipped inside.

CHAPTER 20

**PANAI,
ANDAKAR**

Whack! A cleaver chopped the head off a long fish as several soldiers chattered among themselves, slicing and dicing large bowls of seafood and vegetables. Their curved knives moved with frightening speed as Ryan watched, hidden behind a counter in this industrial-sized kitchen. These guys must be on food detail. And they were cooking a *lot*, which made Ryan wonder how many soldiers were actually stationed here.

He ducked back down, suddenly hit with the realization of how crazy his plan was. He was locked inside this place with who-knew-how-many guys carrying machine guns and knives that looked like they could cut him right in two!

Get a grip, he told himself. Finding his nerve once more, Ryan scurried quickly across the kitchen, hidden from the soldiers' view by the counters. He darted into a hallway, hoping he wouldn't run into anyone.

Fortunately, the hallway was deserted, but Ryan could hear voices just beyond it. He moved closer to the swinging door at the far end, which had a round window in the middle. Ryan guessed the door led to what was once a restaurant and that this was the hallway the waiters used back when it was a working hotel.

Ryan peered out the round window into a huge room that still had the trappings of British Colonial design: dark wood floors, wicker chairs, and palm-leaf fans hanging from the ceiling. But it wasn't a restaurant anymore. One whole wall was lined with computer stations, each manned by a technician wearing a headset. The other wall was filled with sophisticated flat-screen TVs and a sea of flickering, shifting images. Ryan saw maps, newscasts, and a whole bank of monitors showing surveillance-camera footage of the hotel's grounds.

It didn't take a genius to realize the hotel was some kind of command center.

Before Ryan could see more, a movement in

his peripheral vision caught his attention. One of the soldiers was heading right toward him! Ryan bolted back down the hallway. He passed the kitchen door and spotted a staircase just as the door behind him opened. Ryan dodged behind the staircase. He pressed his back against the wall and held his breath, not making a sound.

Hearing the soldier give orders to the kitchen crew, Ryan exhaled in relief: He hadn't been spotted. But the hallway was getting busy now. He had to get out of there. He darted up the stairway to the second floor.

It was much quieter upstairs. Ryan stayed close to the walls as he snuck down the hall, passing doors that opened into what had once been guest rooms. After checking the doorsills to make sure no lights were on, he tried the handles. A few opened to offices. He searched them briefly but found nothing that helped him figure out what this place was. At the end of the hallway, one of the doors opened into a much bigger room. Ryan stepped silently inside.

It was completely dark. Ryan knew he couldn't turn on a light. He used the glow from his cell phone to look around. The room must have been a suite way back when, but it was being used as a storage area now. The walls were lined with shelves stuffed with thousands of file folders.

Ryan pulled one down, careful to remember where he'd found it. On the front of the folder was a red-and-gold shield with a white triangle floating in the middle. It was some sort of logo. Ryan couldn't read the language of the writing underneath it, so he snapped a photo. Maybe later Danny could figure out what it was. He opened it and found a dossier written in a language he didn't understand. A picture of a middle-aged man was clipped inside, along with what appeared to be all his essential information. Ryan could recognize dates and times strewn throughout, but he couldn't read the entries themselves.

Ryan guessed that these were files on Andakar's citizens. With all the communications technology and surveillance equipment he saw downstairs and the files up here, Ryan was pretty certain the hotel was currently the base for some kind of intelligence agency. All the emails Danny found to Ryan's father had come from Panai, and some mentioned Kali Thawar. That meant Myat Kaw could have had access to lots of top secret information. No wonder they wanted to find him.

After putting the folder back, Ryan left the file room and continued down the hall. From the front of the building, someone was yelling, sounding more scared than angry. Creeping closer, Ryan arrived at the end of the hallway. It opened onto a landing that overlooked the old hotel's lobby.

Crouching low, Ryan sidled up to the balcony rail and peered over. The lobby was connected to this upper floor by a wide, gently curving staircase. Down below, two of the blue-uniformed soldiers held a frightened man between them, his desperate cries turning to pleading sobs. An officer stood imperiously before him, questioning the man in a cold, emotionless tone.

Ryan wanted to get a better look, but he couldn't risk being seen. The officer in charge spat out a command and the soldiers dragged the prisoner away, his pleas echoing uselessly. They took him to a stairway on the opposite side of the lobby that led to whatever was downstairs.

Backing carefully away from the rail, Ryan hurried once more toward the staff stairwell. If the soldiers were taking their prisoner to the basement, then maybe Ryan's dad was down there, too.

CHAPTER
21

**PANAI,
ANDAKAR**

The basement was like something out of a horror movie. Half the lights were out or flickering, and the bare concrete walls and underground dampness gave it a cold and threatening atmosphere. There was a stench down here, too, which Ryan thought was probably a combination of filth, body odor, and fear.

A confusing network of corridors ran underneath the building. Ryan didn't think the soldiers used this part of the old hotel much, as he'd passed a couple of forgotten laundry carts and found a closet still packed with rotted-out supplies. He got completely turned around in the hallways, which all looked alike, until he didn't know where he was.

Finally, he spotted a pair of steel doors at the end of yet another hallway. Cautiously, he opened one of the doors and immediately heard the buzz of machinery from the other side. This seemed to be an entrance to a whole other section of the basement housing the generators and equipment that kept the building functioning. Ryan stepped inside, careful not to let the heavy door slam.

A long chamber stretched out before him, lit only by a couple of bare bulbs. Several giant, rusted-out furnaces lined one side of the room. At the far end, a hallway led off into darkness. Through the hum of the machinery, Ryan now noticed other sounds. People's voices, moaning and crying out in desperation.

He started that way, then froze, hearing something else—footsteps. Coming closer quickly. Ryan moved to the furnaces, slipping silently into the shadows between them as a soldier entered from the hallway at the other end of the room. The man passed within a few feet of Ryan but didn't stop. He exited through the steel door and was gone. The moment the door clicked shut, Ryan hurried toward the voices. If his father was here, he could only imagine what condition he might find him in.

Around the corner, he could hear what sounded like an interrogation. The hallway was empty of guards, so Ryan risked a peek through an open doorway. His heart stopped at what he saw inside.

Rusted pipes spanned the ceiling of a long room that once housed the water tanks for the hotel but was now a makeshift torture chamber. Ryan saw a man and a woman chained to the wall with iron manacles. In the middle of the room, Ryan recognized the guy who had been dragged away upstairs, his shirt now off. He was tied to a chair, whimpering. Behind him, the officer raised a riding crop. Ryan flinched as the officer swung, viciously striking the man's exposed back. The man screamed and Ryan turned away, horrified.

Down the hall, Ryan discovered a series of rooms that had been converted into jail cells. He counted six in all, three on each side. There were still no guards in sight. Ryan took the opportunity to look inside each cell.

But his dad wasn't here. The prisoners in the cells were all locals, and they looked miserable. Ryan wished he could help them escape, but that would alert the guards in the interrogation room.

"Hey." Ryan spun around at the whispered voice behind him. A young woman stared out from behind the bars of a cell, her face streaked with dirt and tears. "You have to get out of here."

Ryan's shock turned to surprise at her perfect English. "I'm looking for someone. A man, an American—"

"There's no American here. Go."

"Are you sure? His name is John Quinn—he's helping Myat Kaw."

The young woman's expression changed at the mention of Myat Kaw's name. "You know Myat Kaw?" she asked.

Ryan moved to her, noticing that other faces were now appearing at the cell doors. "John Quinn is my father. He was trying to get Myat Kaw to safety. I have to find him."

One of the other prisoners, an older man, whispered something in their native language. The young woman listened, then translated for Ryan. "He says he knows your father. That he's very brave."

Ryan turned to the man, trying to keep his voice down despite the excitement he was feeling. "Do you know where he is?" The man shook his head, then spoke once more to the young woman. He went on for some time and Ryan couldn't help feeling impatient, hearing the cries from the interrogation just around the corner. He didn't have much time.

"There is a student at the Panai Teaching College," she said. "His name is Ashin Myek. He says to ask this student. He may know where your father went."

"How does he know?"

"Many of us helped Myat Kaw." They both turned at the sound of a door swinging open around the corner. Her eyes met his in fear, "You must go—hurry!"

Ryan's hand went to the lock on her cell. "I'll let you out—all of you."

"No," she whispered. "This is Andakar—there is nowhere to go, and it is worse for those who run. *Go! Save yourself!*"

Ryan hesitated, but he could hear the soldiers dragging their mumbling prisoner toward the cells. He took off, racing for the steel door, frustrated at not being able to do more for the people who had helped him.

Making it through the steel door, Ryan raced for the stairs, more intent on speed than on stealth at this point. But the corridors were confusing, and Ryan's rush ended with him getting hopelessly lost. He tried to backtrack, but couldn't tell one hallway from the other. Frustrated and annoyed with himself, he turned a corner and came face-to-face with one of the soldiers!

Ryan and the soldier were equally startled, but Ryan was the first to recover. As the soldier went for his pistol, Ryan brought a knee up into the guy's stomach! The soldier doubled over, gasping for breath.

Unlike the fight at school, Ryan didn't have to be careful and pull his punches. He was a couple of inches shorter than the soldier, but he delivered a Palm Heel Strike that sent the man to his knees. The soldier raised his gun, but Ryan grabbed it and dealt one final Hammer Fist Punch that sent him to the ground, unconscious.

Ryan could hardly believe what he'd done. His body had reacted instinctively, all those years of practice paying off in a big way. But after seeing the way these soldiers tortured people, he didn't feel bad at all. He ran up the stairs, the gun still in his hand.

At the top, Ryan paused to make sure no one was around, and then went out the back door. He darted across the expanse of lawn, keeping to the shadows as he raced for the back gate.

There weren't any palm trees on this side to climb, so he had to find another way out.

Ryan crept along the back wall, getting closer to the gate. Two soldiers were stationed at the entrance, one along the road and the other inside the guard shack. Ryan still had the gun, but he didn't even know how to use it. Out of options, he raised the weapon, hoping he could fake enough confidence to force the soldier to open the gate. He took a step forward, but the night suddenly erupted with shouts from the main building.

An alarm was being raised! The soldier he'd hit must have come around. The man in the guard shack came out and joined his comrade on the road. They both looked quizzically toward the hotel. This was the only opportunity Ryan was going to get. Slipping inside the guard shack, he searched for the button to open the gate. Spotting one with an icon of an open door on its face, he pressed it and hurried back out.

Hearing the metal gates creak open, the two soldiers whirled around. Before they could raise their machine guns, Ryan fired two shots into the air, high over their heads, but loud enough to make them both duck for cover. Without a backward glance, he squeezed through the gate.

Ryan sprinted down the street as a siren began to wail from the compound. He was out, but they would soon be hot on his trail.

CHAPTER

22

**PANAI,
ANDAKAR**

Stopping to catch his breath, Ryan looked back over his shoulder. He'd been running for blocks, making sharp turns, going down alleys, anything he could think of to shake the men chasing him. But there were too many. Every time he thought he was in the clear, they'd appear once more, cutting off his escape.

The streets he'd taken had been dark, with virtually no electric lights on anywhere. But a block away, he spotted a busier area with bright lights, noise, and people. Ryan had hoped he could lose the soldiers by hiding in the shadows, but that wasn't working. Needing a new plan, he headed toward the crowd.

Old-fashioned neon signs assaulted Ryan from both sides of the street. The garish colors and blinking lights reminded him of a carnival. Locals were everywhere, eating, drinking, and chatting at a variety of small cafés and food stands. Dressed in jeans and T-shirts, they didn't look that different from people hanging out anywhere else in the world.

Ryan slowed down and tried to blend in, but being the only American around, he stood out in the crowd. Still, he received hesitant smiles from most of the people he passed as he made his way to the far end of the street. He nodded and smiled back. The distraction almost got him caught.

Ryan stopped short. Less than thirty feet ahead, blue-uniformed soldiers shoved people out of the way. A woman was pushed to the ground, but the soldiers just stepped right over her. Ryan lowered his head and turned around. Moving as quickly as he could without rousing suspicion, he headed back the way he'd come. He didn't get far before he saw another group of soldiers fanning out as they roughly pushed their way through the crowd from the opposite end.

Ryan was trapped.

Desperate, he looked frantically for an escape route. He stood in front of a crowded café open to the street, where patrons sat at plastic tables so low to the ground they seemed better suited for little kids than adults. The soldiers closed in from both sides, and Ryan made his move.

Three men looked up in surprise as Ryan plopped himself down in a red plastic chair opposite them. "Hi," he said, keeping his back to the sidewalk.

The men exchanged curious looks. One of them looked toward the door and his expression darkened. Out of the corner of his eye, Ryan could see the blue uniform of a soldier on the sidewalk. The man spoke a few words to his friends, and they saw the soldier as well. Their gazes all turned to Ryan.

Were they going to give him up? Ryan tried not to let the anxiety show on his face, but he knew if they did, he'd be toast. Glancing down, he had a sudden inspiration. He loosened the string bracelet the monk had given him at the Ashoka Temple. Taking it off his wrist, he took the hand of the man across from him.

"Tasmati ca niva," Ryan said, trying to imitate the sounds of the words the monk had spoken to him.

For a breathless moment, Ryan thought the stranger was going to jerk his hand away. Instead, a smile spread across his face.

"Tin ba dai," he replied.

One of the other men suddenly laughed, throwing an arm out and draping it over Ryan's shoulder in a fatherly fashion. The other two joined in, smiling as if nothing was out of the ordinary and talking loudly among themselves once more.

Ryan couldn't understand a word, but he nodded as if he belonged here. He could practically feel the eyes of the soldier on the back of his head.

After a moment, the men's chatter subsided as they looked beyond him. One of them nodded to him, his face serious. Ryan checked, and, sure enough, the soldier had moved on. The man next to him pointed toward the back of the café, making it clear Ryan should leave that way.

Ryan thanked them again and then weaved his way out through the crowded tables. A long hallway led past the kitchen, where the smell of curry and garlic made him realize how hungry he was.

Ryan pushed open the door at the back, disappearing quickly into the night.

CHAPTER
23

**NEW YORK,
USA**

An airborne French fry smacked into Danny's laptop screen. The guys at the table behind him were goofing off, but he didn't have time to get distracted. Cleaning the greasy smear with his T-shirt, he went back to reading.

The school cafeteria wasn't the best place to be researching the most feared military dictatorship in Southeast Asia, but Danny didn't have much choice. History class started in twenty minutes, and he was using every spare second to help Ryan.

So far, he'd managed to locate sixteen blog posts written by Myat Kaw. They were difficult to find because the website where they were originally posted had been shut down. Danny assumed Andakar's government was responsible for that, hoping to limit the damage Myat Kaw was causing. Fortunately, people who cared about Andakar's future had copied the posts before they were removed and put them up on other sites.

Danny was seriously impressed by what he read. He suspected Myat Kaw might be a world-class hacker who had infiltrated Andakar's most secure networks. That would explain how this anonymous blogger had access to information the military dictatorship desperately wanted to remain secret. There were reports of Andakar covertly purchasing missiles from the Chinese that had made headlines around the world, proof that some German tourists had mysteriously gone missing, and an exposé of the lavish lifestyle enjoyed by Andakar's top generals while much of the country went hungry. The revelations in the blog posts were creating huge problems for the government. Myat Kaw was doing what no one had been able to accomplish for over thirty years—making the country's iron-fisted rulers sweat.

"Daniel." Danny looked up to find Principal Milankovic approaching his table. With nimble fingers, he cleared his screen, replacing Myat Kaw's blog posts with a map of the thirteen colonies. "Have you spoken to Ryan in the last couple of days?"

"Um, yeah—he's really sick."

"That's too bad." The principal regarded Danny with skepticism. "The school emailed his parents but didn't get any response. You're sure they're not off somewhere?"

"No, sir." Danny tried his best to sound convincing. "He has the flu—the *Samoan* flu. So does his mom, supercontagious. Ryan's dad is spending all his time taking care of them."

"The Samoan flu?" Principal Milankovic raised his eyebrows.

Danny had a feeling he'd gone too far, but he couldn't back down now. "Fever, hives—not pretty. Trust me, you're glad he's not here."

The principal nodded. "If you speak to him, please have Ryan remind his parents that the school needs to be notified about all absences."

"Will do, sir! I'm sure it's just an oversight." Danny waited until Principal Milankovic was out of the cafeteria, then grabbed his backpack from under the table. He pulled out John Quinn's laptop and flipped the cover open. One email excuse from Ryan's dad, coming up!

As he was typing, Kasey sat in the chair next to him. "Hey, Danny, whatcha doing?" Danny slammed the lid closed. Smooth, he chided himself, very subtle.

"Nothing much. Just hanging."

"Two laptops? Isn't that a lot, even for you?"

"Sometimes I'm just too much for one computer to handle!"

Kasey laughed. "I bet you are."

So often, Danny didn't know where the cocky things he said came from. He certainly wasn't as confident inside as he acted. The truth was, for years he had felt much more comfortable lost inside digital worlds—video games, the web, challenging hacks—and so he didn't even bother much with Real Life. When he was younger, that had worked well for him. At the small elementary school he attended, Danny had only a couple of friends and spent most of his free time alone.

But everything changed in middle school. Suddenly, he had to deal with an eclectic variety of students in a school with well over a thousand kids. Danny had been overwhelmed at first, not fitting into any particular group and not really knowing how to make friends. People seemed to look right past him, hardly noticing he was even there. He'd had a few tough months and then, one night as he was listening to The Cure's "Just Like Heaven," Danny decided he'd had enough of being ignored.

Taking down his concert poster of Robert Smith, the eccentric and brilliant lead singer of The Cure, Danny had gone to his bathroom. He grabbed a tube of hair gel and squirted a glob of it into his hand. Looking between the poster and his own reflected image, Danny spiked his hair up in every direction just like his musician hero. It was wild, but he loved it. Whoever this new kid looking back at him in the mirror was, Danny liked him.

The next morning, he ripped a few strategic holes in his jeans, then put on a T-shirt and a burgundy sport coat his mom had made him buy for the occasional opera they attended. Danny slipped out of the apartment before his mom saw him, and headed to school, excited but scared.

Nobody had ignored him, that's for sure. For the first time, people paid attention. It wasn't always good—Danny got picked on some, the way anybody does who's different. But he also met some interesting kids who'd never really noticed him before. He wasn't entirely comfortable in his new role, but he faked the confidence he didn't feel. Danny started making friends for the first time. It wasn't until he and Ryan connected a couple of months ago, though, that he found someone he could totally relax with and just be himself. He never had to put on an act with Ryan. And now that his best friend was in trouble, Danny was going to do anything he could to help.

"So I texted Ryan a couple of times, but I didn't get any response," Kasey said. "Is everything all right?"

"He's sick."

"Too sick to answer a text?"

"His, um, hands are *swollen*. You should see his thumbs—they're like cucumbers."

Kasey wasn't buying it. "Look, if he doesn't want to go to the dance with me, I'm not gonna be mad or anything."

"He asked you to the dance?" That was news to Danny.

"No, I asked him. He didn't tell you? I thought you were his best friend."

"I am, yeah, but he's been superbusy lately—and sick. Really, really sick."

Kasey seemed genuinely disappointed. "Whatever. He doesn't want to go. It's fine—

but he doesn't have to avoid me." She stood as Danny's phone dinged with a text message. He opened it instantly when he saw it was from Ryan. "That's him, isn't it? Guess his cucumber thumbs suddenly got better."

"Kasey, wait—it's not what you think." Danny glanced at Ryan's text, a photo of a red-and-gold shield with a white pyramid floating over it and the message: *Can you find out what this is?*

"It's okay. Maybe my brother is right about you two. I just thought you guys were different. Tell Ryan not to bother about the dance. I'll ask somebody else."

She turned to go when Danny blurted out, "His dad's missing, his mom's been kidnapped, and Ryan used a fake ID to sneak into one of the most dangerous countries on earth!" Danny was surprised by his own outburst. "So he's been a little busy."

Kasey stared at him a beat. "Wow. When you lie for someone, you really go for it, don't you?"

But Danny's expression was serious. "I know it sounds crazy. I wish I was lying."

CHAPTER
24

PANAI,
ANDAKAR

A re you insane?" Tasha got right in Ryan's face. "You could've gotten yourself killed!"

She'd been waiting for him when he snuck back in the window and was reading him the riot act. Ryan knew she had a point, but he didn't like being treated like a child. "I didn't get killed. Or caught. And I got information we can use."

"A name of some random person who *might* know something about your father, given to you by a stranger in a jail cell."

"It's more than you've found."

Tasha looked like she wanted to clobber him, but Ryan stood his ground. They stared each other down a moment, and then she turned away, struggling to get her temper in check. "You said he's a student?"

"At the Panai Teaching College. Ashin Myek."

"And how do we contact him?" Tasha asked.

"I don't know."

"Where does he live? Does he have a phone number we can call? An email address—anything?"

Ryan realized it wasn't much to go on. "We can check at the college. They must have a directory or something."

Tasha looked out the window past the fire escape. "And you're sure you weren't followed?"

"Positive," Ryan said. "I was careful—that's why it took so long."

Unfortunately, he had more bad news for her. While he was hiding out, Danny had sent him the information he'd uncovered on the logo Ryan had found at the hotel. "This hotel where I went, it's run by the Army Services Intelligence division."

"The ASI? You snuck into a command center for the ASI?" To his surprise, Tasha laughed. "You really *are* insane."

"I didn't know what it was when I went in."

"Well, let me educate you. The ASI is one of

the most feared, hated, and ruthless spy agencies in the world."

"I saw what they're capable of," Ryan said, remembering the brutality of the riding crop striking the prisoner's bare back. "They torture people."

"They do worse than that. They learned from the KGB and China's MSS. And now, they've probably captured your handsome face on numerous security cameras. Congratulations—by tomorrow, you'll be the most wanted man in Andakar."

Ryan leaned against the wall and slid to the floor. Tasha was probably right; with all the monitors he'd seen at the compound, at least one of them likely got a good image of him. His fake identity would be blown soon, and he had no other way to travel. The half-finished puppets hanging around the workshop seemed to stare at him, taunting. Who was he kidding? There was no way he could pull this off. He was in way over his head.

"You need to sleep." Tasha's tone had shifted, becoming gentler. "The adrenaline's wearing off. You're exhausted."

"I'm fine," Ryan muttered, knowing it was a lie.

"Will you just shut up and do what I say for

a change?" She came over, grabbing some of the fabric as she approached. As she had done for herself, Tasha bunched it into a ball. Forcing Ryan to lie on the floor, she placed it under his head like a pillow. "You're no use to anyone like this."

"I can't . . ." Ryan protested. But he never finished, falling instantly into a deep slumber.

CHAPTER
25

**PANAI,
ANDAKAR**

Tasha had been busy.

Since Ryan had zonked out a few hours ago, she had gathered materials to create disguises, found some food, and even tracked down an address for Ashin Myek. She had thought hard about taking the opportunity to ditch Ryan. But the kid had actually done pretty well by getting them a name. He might still prove useful.

She shook him awake, and he stirred groggily. "Rise and shine. Unless you want to hang around here and wait for me all day."

Ryan sat up, rubbing his eyes, his mop of brown hair sticking out in all directions. He looked outside. "It's morning."

"Your powers of observation are astonishing. Here, eat this. And drink the tea, whether you like it or not. Your body needs it." She set down a bowl of cold noodles and a wooden cup of steaming, cloudy tea. Ryan gulped a large bite of noodles and made a face.

"Those are awful," he said.

"They flavor them with fish sauce."

"For breakfast?"

"It's an acquired taste. But it's all we've got, so eat up." Tasha held out a long cotton shirt and one of the traditional sarongs Ryan had seen on the streets of Panai. "When you're finished, change into these. You'll have to leave your backpack. Put your clothes and high-tops into one of the cloth bags."

Ryan took the sarong. "But this is a skirt."

"And you're man enough to wear it well," she teased. "They'll be looking for an American teenager, so we'll hide you in plain sight. You'll look like a local." At the workshop table, she held up a jar of black liquid. "I found some acrylic paint. We're dyeing your hair, too."

Tasha observed Ryan's confusion as he wrapped the sarong around his waist, trying to figure out how it worked. "Don't tell me in all your travels, you've never worn a sarong?"

Ryan looked at her with concern. "I get to keep my underwear on, right?"

"That depends on how wild and funky you're feeling. But yeah, keeping it on is probably a good idea."

When he'd finished the noodles, Tasha pulled on a pair of plastic gloves, and they got busy dyeing Ryan's hair at the sink. As she worked the black liquid through his untamed mane, he admitted, "I nearly got caught last night."

Tasha tugged his hair roughly, eliciting a yelp of pain. "Would've served you right for sneaking out."

"The only reason I got away is because these strangers helped me—some prisoners at the ASI headquarters and then three men at one of the cafés. They didn't have to."

"You seem surprised. The citizens here hate the ASI."

"But they could've been killed. Why would they risk getting caught?"

"Life is full of risk. Sometimes doing what's right is the riskiest move of all." Tasha picked up a paintbrush. "Now shut up and let me concentrate."

Thirty minutes later, they left through the back door. Considering their limitations, Tasha thought she'd done a good job disguising Ryan. Wearing the traditional sarong, long shirt, and sandals, he definitely looked less American. The acrylic paint had turned his hair jet-black. Not as natural as she would have liked, but it helped him blend in a little better.

Tasha had ditched the red wig and sewn a simple, floor-length skirt for herself from fabric she'd found in the workshop. It covered her feet, which allowed her to wear pants and boots hidden underneath. She wrapped an embroidered silk scarf around her head, covering her hair.

"Look down as much as possible so people can't see your face," she told Ryan.

"Are we going to the college?"

"Yes, but we have to hurry. We need to catch Ashin Myek before he leaves his apartment."

"How did you find him?" Ryan asked, as they crossed the street.

"I called my contact. He sent me everything he could dig up on short notice."

Ryan grinned. "Thought you said it wasn't safe to get in touch with your contact until ten this morning? Sounds like I'm not the only one who breaks the rules."

Tasha could see that some food, a few hours of sleep, and a real lead to follow had done Ryan a world of good. He was less anxious this morning, more sure of himself.

She was actually starting to like this kid. Which was a shame.

It made her *real* mission that much harder.

CHAPTER
26

**PANAI,
ANDAKAR**

The Panai Teaching College was in the midst of a celebration of some kind. Ryan could see over a hundred students gathered in the sprawling courtyard of the main building. Some were dancing to traditional music, while others waved banners and twirled paper umbrellas. The plaza was boisterous and busy, a riot of color and noise.

"That's where Ashin Myek lives," Tasha said, pointing to a plain, two-story building at the edge of campus. Students were leaving and walking toward the festival. She held up her cell phone and showed him a photo. Ashin was in his mid-20s with a gaunt face, high forehead, and bushy hair.

"We have to be careful," Ryan said. "The prisoners at the Kali Thawar told me the ASI was rounding up anyone they suspected of being connected to Myat Kaw."

They found a bench that afforded a view of the building and sat, watching students make their way to the plaza. Ryan was having trouble getting used to the sarong, which was wrapped around his waist and knotted in front. He shifted his legs, uncomfortable and not knowing how to sit so it didn't fall open. After fifteen minutes, Ryan's patience was wearing thin. "Maybe we should just go inside and see if he's home?"

Tasha suddenly stood. "There."

Ryan joined her, slinging the cloth bag with his clothes, shoes, and phone over his shoulder. Following Tasha, he spotted Ashin walking with a couple of friends toward the festival. They laughed together over some private joke.

As they closed in, Ryan noticed a man in a dark suit strolling several feet behind Ashin. The cut of the suit and the way the man carried himself reminded Ryan of Aung Win back in New York. He grabbed Tasha's elbow, holding her back.

"What? We're gonna lose him."

"He's not alone." Ryan nodded subtly toward

the man in the suit and Tasha followed his gaze. The moment she saw him, she understood.

Her eyes expertly swept the area. "Another over there."

And Ryan had just noticed a third, this one dressed more casually, but as laser focused on Ashin as the guy in the suit. "At least three of them."

"Come on." Tasha started moving again, keeping pace with Ashin and the men trailing him, but holding back so they weren't seen.

Ryan tried to keep the desperation out of his voice but didn't quite succeed. "We have to talk to him. He's the only person who may know where my dad is."

"We will," Tasha said.

Ashin and his friends made it to the festival, standing together. Revelers in traditional costumes of richly embroidered silk danced to the beat of drums. Huge papier-mâché elephants dotted the crowd. Neon green and psychedelic pink, they bounced and boogied beside others outfitted with more ceremonial Asian decorations. It took Ryan a moment to realize that there were people inside the giant elephants. At least two or three students were hidden under each costume.

Tasha positioned them in the middle of a small crowd of onlookers who were cheering on the dancing elephants. "They're not moving in, just keeping him under surveillance." She looked from Ashin to the ASI agents, calculating a strategy. "If they stay in the crowd, maybe I can get close enough to talk to him."

"But if the ASI suspects anything, they'll pull him in. Probably torture him like that guy I saw. You, too."

Tasha's uncertainty was apparent; she knew this wasn't a good plan. "Like you said, we don't have any other leads and we're running out of time."

She began to move closer to Ashin, when Ryan stopped her. "Wait, I've got a better idea." Before Tasha could protest, he grabbed her hand and pulled her in the opposite direction. Annoyed, she had no choice but to follow.

Just behind the crowd, Ryan had spotted another of the beautiful elephant costumes—only this one was sitting on two wood tables, supporting it from head to tail. Ryan scanned the area, but everyone's attention was focused on the parade. Nobody was paying any attention to the elephant costume.

"You're the butt," he whispered. She glared

at him and he realized what he'd said. "I mean, you're *in* the butt—no, that's not—just take the back, okay?" She rolled her eyes, then nodded.

Keeping low so they didn't attract attention, Ryan pulled back the decorative panels that formed the elephant's body. Tasha dipped underneath, disappearing inside the elephant's torso and Ryan followed. Inside the papier-mâché elephant, it was hot and humid. Ryan discovered that sections of the costume, which had appeared solid from the outside, were actually made of a mesh material that he could see through. It was kind of like looking through a window screen.

Two wooden handles came down from the top of the elephant's head. Ryan grabbed them, glancing over his shoulder to see that Tasha had hold of another handle in the back that held up the tail end. He gave her the signal and they carefully lifted the elephant.

"Who's the thief now?" she said.

Ryan guided them around and into the crowd. Seeing through the mesh made walking challenging, and he bumped into a couple of students as he figured it out. One of them spun around in anger at being hit, but broke into a grin as he saw the elephant head looming over him.

"Dance, *rahu*, dance!" he yelled. The student began to bob and weave, leaving Ryan no choice but to dance with him, moving the handles up-and-down, then side-to-side, creating a rhythmic motion.

"Really?" Tasha whispered.

"All the other elephants are *dancing*. You want me to blend in, don't you?" Ryan moved forward once more, feeling uncoordinated as he walked and controlled the elephant at the same time. Up ahead, he caught sight of Ashin and his friends and maneuvered in his direction. Festivalgoers parted for the elephant, giving Ryan a straight shot at their target.

"We won't have much time," Tasha advised. "Get close and I'll grab him. Work your way deeper into the crowd—the busier, the better."

"Got it." Ryan spotted one of the ASI agents several feet behind Ashin. He navigated so that the elephant's body was between the agent and Ashin, blocking his view, then spat out, "Now!"

Holding the tail handle with one hand, Tasha timed her movements perfectly, reaching out and grabbing Ashin as they passed. Ashin stumbled but managed to stay on his feet, shocked to find himself suddenly inside the elephant. Panic filled his eyes until Tasha whispered, "We're friends of Myat Kaw—keep walking!"

Ryan slowed his pace, giving Ashin an opportunity to get in step with them. "You can't be here," Ashin warned. "I'm being followed!"

Tasha tried to sound comforting. "We know. We just need information. We're trying to find John Quinn—do you know where he is?"

Ryan glanced to his left and suddenly saw the looming figure of one of the ASI agents right beside them. He was searching the crowd and talking into a handheld radio. The man seemed to look right at Ryan, who held his breath as he swerved away. Ryan knew the agent couldn't see inside the costume, but he was unsettled anyway.

Ashin spoke urgently. "I don't know where John is now. I left my car for him several days ago and gave him directions to the village of Thanlin. That was the last I heard of him."

"How far is Thanlin?" Ryan asked, making a wide circle through the crowd.

"Four or five hours depending on how many times the bus breaks down. In the mountains." Ashin looked through the mesh as his friends came back into view, Ryan's circle having brought them around once more. "Good luck!"

As they passed close to his friends, Ashin ducked back out, laughing joyously as if it had all been a lark. His friends laughed with him, making a convincing show of it. Ryan saw one of the ASI agents look at the elephant, then glance down toward Ryan's feet. Ryan could only hope that seeing his sandals and sarong would be enough to convince the agent that nothing was wrong.

Ryan steered the elephant back to where they found it. Two students saw them approaching and were furious, gesticulating wildly and cursing at them. For once, Ryan was happy he didn't speak the language as the owners continued to scold them. Ryan and Tasha placed the costume back on the wood tables and hurried off as the students railed at them.

Moving away from the crowd, Ryan couldn't help smiling at Tasha. "We make a pretty good team, huh?"

She didn't even glance his direction. "I don't do teams."

CHAPTER 27

NANSANG PROVINCE, ANDAKAR

Ryan pulled the paper bag to his mouth, puking for the third time as the rickety bus careened around yet another hairpin turn. By this point, though, he didn't have anything left to heave. The combination of noxious fumes and erratic motion had kept him nauseated since they first started their ascent into the mountains.

The bus was in terrible shape, rattling and spewing gray-black exhaust as it struggled up the incline, gears grinding in complaint at every turn. Ryan couldn't stop glancing out the window, his stomach churning every time he saw the steep drop from the road's edge. He could see straight down to the bottom of a watery chasm hundreds of feet below.

"Why do they go so fast?" he asked Tasha. She barely seemed to notice the wild ride, eyes closed as she tried to nap. "If the bus goes over the cliff, they're gonna die, too."

"They're Buddhists. They believe in karma and rebirth. The drivers figure if we go over, they'll just come back in their next life as something better."

"Great."

They had been traveling for hours. The farther they got from the city, the more rural the area became. Factories were replaced by vast fields of sugarcane and rice paddies. Ryan couldn't help but notice the extreme poverty in which most of the citizens of Andakar lived. Their homes were simple, with wood walls and rusted-out, corrugated metal roofs. Oxen mingled freely with villagers, and barefoot children in threadbare clothes ran alongside the bus, waving. Ryan smiled and waved back. No matter how tough things were, kids always found ways to play.

But as the bus lumbered through the mountains, Ryan had little to smile about. Two hours of twisting and turning made him a wreck. He tried distracting himself with the deck of cards, practicing his sleight-of-hand techniques, but even that didn't work.

"Where are we now?" he asked Tasha.

"Nansang Province. It continues over the mountain range and down to Andakar's border with Thailand."

Ryan remembered the CIA agents in New York showing his mom those photos of his dad. They said he met with smugglers in Muang Tak, Thailand. So maybe his father had used the smugglers to sneak him into Andakar from Thailand? It made sense that he'd return by the same route once he had Myat Kaw. But things must have gone wrong somewhere along the way.

A short while later, Tasha sat up, looking out the window. "We're here—this is Thanlin. Ashin gave your dad directions to this village, which means it probably wasn't part of his original plan."

"Are there any friends of ours here?" The bus jerked to a stop, engine clattering as it died. Ryan, Tasha, and a couple of locals stood, making their way to the front.

"None that I know of," Tasha said. "Don't talk to anyone. I'll take a look around, see if there's anyone I trust enough to ask a few discreet questions."

"What am I supposed to do?"

"Nothing. Got it?" There was no room for argument.

"Got it," Ryan agreed.

Getting off the bus, Ryan quickly tossed his puke-filled bag into the trash. He took a gulp from his water bottle, rinsing out his mouth, then finished the rest. Tasha took off down the street, doing her best imitation of a tourist.

Ryan wandered through the center of the village. It was mostly comprised of little houses with walls made from tightly woven strands of bamboo and thatched roofs. The scenery surrounding it was breathtaking, though. Thanlin was perched on a hillside with sweeping views of the jungle in every direction.

He sat on a ledge and opened his knapsack. Digging to the bottom, Ryan found his last thin box of chocolate treats. The chocolate was probably soft and squishy from the heat, but he didn't care. As he brought the box out, his hand grazed the folded photo of his family.

He wasn't sure if looking at it would give him renewed determination or just make him depressed, but he took it out anyway. As he opened it, he realized that he was being watched.

Trying to act casual, Ryan looked up. A few feet away stood a cute little girl in a Hello Kitty T-shirt, with long black hair and smudges across her nose. She was very curious and pointed at the box of candy in his hand. Ryan held it up.

"This? Yeah, they're really good." He opened the box and pulled out a long stick that was actually a cookie, most of it covered with delicious chocolate. "It's called a pocky stick. It's from Japan. The chocolate's yummy."

Ryan took a bite of the pocky, showing her how tasty it was. He knew the girl probably didn't understand a word he said, but he figured chocolate was a universal language. He pulled another stick out of the box and held it out. "You can try one, if you want."

The girl's eyes got big as she took it from him. She crunched into it with gusto, chomping down until it was gone. Before she finished swallowing the last bite, she was ready for another one. Ryan noticed a few more kids watching from a short distance away and handed her the whole box. "Take it all," he said, then gestured to her friends. "But you have to share, okay?"

The girl nodded eagerly, taking the box. She paused, noticing the photo Ryan had set on the ledge next to him. Her expression clouded as she looked at it. Ryan picked it up, so she could see it better.

"Do you recognize him? This man?" He pointed to his dad and she nodded. Ryan pointed between the picture and himself. "He's my father. Have you seen him?"

The girl took the photo, looking between it and Ryan. Abruptly, she turned and walked away. Ryan grabbed his bag and followed. "Wait—I need that."

She kept going, not looking back. One of the other children suddenly called to the little girl, and she spun around. All of them were instantly on alert, their attention focused toward the entrance to the village. Only now did Ryan hear the sound of approaching vehicles as the kids scattered in all directions.

"Hey!" he called, as the little girl took off running.

But she didn't slow down. Ryan was normally pretty fast, but in the sarong and sandals, he felt clumsy and uncoordinated. As he ran, he noticed villagers hurrying to their homes and disappearing inside. The girl turned the corner, and Ryan lost sight of her.

As he came around the bend, he spotted her

on a rocky path along the cliff's edge. "Please!" he called, when she looked back at him. "I need that picture!" But she took off once more along the path toward a group of trees.

Ryan kicked off his sandals and put on a burst of speed as he sprinted away from the village. It was much easier to run like this, and he closed the distance quickly. As the little girl vanished into the undergrowth, Ryan was only a few steps behind. Bursting through the trees, he stopped, looking around to see which direction she had gone.

Which is when a man's hand reached around from behind him, covering Ryan's mouth and jerking him backward!

CHAPTER 28

**THANLIN,
ANDAKAR**

Quiet!" Ryan strained to break free as the man spun him around. He was surprised to see the Hello Kitty girl right behind him. The man whispered fiercely, "If anyone sees us talking, my daughter and I will be in great danger."

The girl looked up at Ryan with big brown eyes.

"You understand?" the man asked. Ryan nodded, relaxing enough that the man finally let go.

The girl held out the photo to the man, who studied it, and then looked at Ryan warily. "Who are you?" he demanded.

"Ryan Quinn. That's my father. You know him?"

The man was short, but powerfully built with deeply bronzed skin. His daughter cuddled into his side, and he placed a protective arm around her. She clutched the box of pocky sticks tightly to her chest, her eyes never leaving Ryan.

"He came several days ago," the man told Ryan, handing him back the photo. "He needed to get out of the country. I sometimes take English and European tourists on expeditions into the jungles, so he asked for my help."

"Was he okay? Nobody's heard from him in almost a week." Ryan couldn't stop the flood of questions. "Did you take him somewhere? Do you know where he is?"

"He didn't want me to go with him. I gave him directions to the border. He was fine when he left. But others came looking for him. Soldiers from the ASI."

"Did they find him?"

"I don't know." The man's tone was grave. "There were many of them."

Ryan's heart sank, but he refused to believe the worst until he knew for sure. "Where did he go?"

"Up the mountain and through the jungle. At the top of Mount Bana there is a holy place—the Mae Wong Temples. There are places to hide in the temples—secret chambers known only to the villagers of Thanlin. I hoped he might be safe there."

"Can you take me?"

"You're just a boy—you could never make it. And if the ASI find out I helped you—or your father—they will come after my family."

Ryan didn't want to put anyone else at risk, but he had to do something. "If my dad made it there, then I will, too."

They were interrupted by a shout: "Ryan!" It was Tasha, her tone urgent. Ryan hurried out of the trees and saw her searching for him along the rocky path.

"Tasha! I found someone—"

But she didn't let him finish. "They're here. Two trucks of ASI soldiers just pulled in. Come on!"

Suddenly, a shot rang out and Tasha dropped to the ground. Ryan ducked back, terrified she had been hit. He glanced behind him. The villager had taken the girl's hand and was moving deeper into the trees. Ryan looked between the man and where Tasha had fallen, not knowing what to do.

Then, Tasha stood and scrambled behind one of the big rocks. She was okay—she hadn't been shot! But ASI soldiers appeared, cutting her off from Ryan and the trees. Tasha looked at him across the expanse with a fierce expression. Ryan had the weirdest feeling that she actually seemed *angry*.

Another gunshot reverberated through the canyon, and Tasha had no choice—she raced off in the opposite direction, away from Ryan. They were now separated by a squadron of soldiers with rifles. But Ryan couldn't afford to even think about that. If he lost sight of the villager and the girl, he'd also lose any chance of finding his dad.

He cut back through the trees, only to find that the man was already far ahead. "Wait!" Ryan yelled, his bare feet stinging with every step.

The man didn't slow down until his daughter pulled his arm, urging him to stop. It was just enough time for Ryan to catch up. "Please—at least tell me which way to go."

The man's focus was on getting to safety. "There is no time. If they catch us helping you, they will kill us."

"You're the only chance I have of finding my father." Ryan didn't even try to keep the desperation from his tone.

The man wavered, then let out a heavy sigh. "There is a path—easy to follow, but difficult to climb. It will take you down from Thanlin and up Mount Bana on the other side."

"Can you show me?"

The man debated with himself a moment more, then turned to the girl. He spoke to her in their language and she nodded. "This way," he said to Ryan.

Ryan started after him, then turned back briefly. "Thank you," he said to the girl.

She held out the box of candy and repeated, "Thank you."

Ryan hurried to catch up with the villager. Behind him, he heard soldiers shouting and the roar of more vehicles arriving. He had no idea what lay ahead, but he knew there was no turning back.

Ryan was now completely on his own.

CHAPTER
29

**NEW YORK,
USA**

*E*ver since Kasey learned what was going on with Ryan and his parents, all she'd thought about was how she could help. Before their walk downtown, Kasey had tried to talk to Ryan a few times during their classes, but hadn't had much luck. He was quiet around her, but she could tell there was something special about him. And she'd been right. Their conversation had been so great. True, she really didn't know him that well yet. But she'd sensed a real connection, like they'd been friends for years. When they talked, it didn't feel like he was interested in her because he thought she was popular but because he cared about what she thought.

Kasey and Danny had met up after school yesterday, and he had shown her what he found in New York's property records database. Danny had tracked down three buildings around the city that were owned by companies with ties to Andakar's military regime. One of them was a warehouse pretty close to their school.

She had convinced Danny they should go investigate the buildings themselves, and he had finally agreed. They were standing across the street from the warehouse now, but they didn't have much time before school started. Kasey had lied to her dad, telling him she was heading in early for a rehearsal. She hated lying to him, but she figured it was for a good cause. With three older brothers and a single father who had raised them all, Kasey had been treated like a breakable doll her whole life. She loved her family but felt increasingly suffocated by them. The Stieglitz men still saw her as a little girl they needed to protect. Well, she was done with that.

"I'm going in," she told Danny.

Danny lowered his camera and looked at her like she was nuts. "You can't just walk in there— these guys have guns!"

"What else are we gonna do? Call the police?"

"I told you, we can't," Danny said. "That Aung Win dude said he'd kill Mrs. Quinn if Ryan told the cops."

"But the police know how to handle this kind of thing. We don't."

"It's not up to us—it's Ryan's call. He thinks if he finds his dad, then he'll know what to do."

"Well, we can't see anything from out here," Kasey said.

They looked back at the warehouse across the street. It was a brick fortress, square and flat with no windows, bearing a sign across the top that read: Assured Moving and Storage. The front door was gated, and a large, rolling metal door for trucks had been closed since they arrived.

"How would you get inside?" Danny asked. "It looks pretty sealed up. We can't just go in through the front door."

"Actually," Kasey said, "that's exactly what we're going to do. Switch the camera to video. I'll ring the bell and see if I can angle it to shoot inside."

"That sounds like a *terrible* plan." Danny went ahead and put the tiny camera in video mode.

"You got a better one?"

"Nope. But that doesn't make yours good."

Kasey took the camera, knowing he was right. She crossed the street, thinking of clever things to say that might get her inside. She could pretend she was a Girl Scout selling cookies—or maybe she should tell them she was working on a school report about the Lower East Side? Those both sounded kind of lame, but they might work. People often underestimated Kasey, assuming she wasn't very smart because she was pretty. Truth was that Kasey was curious about almost everything: How things worked, why people acted the way they did, what other people's lives were like.

Just as she was about to ring the front bell, the metal garage door made a grating sound and began to lift. Thinking fast, Kasey walked right past, stopping instead at the next building down, which was under construction and surrounded by scaffolding. She hid behind a beam and watched as the garage door slowly opened. A truck rolled out and idled on the edge of the sidewalk.

Across the street, Danny silently motioned her to stay hidden and safe. But Kasey knew this could be the only chance they had to see inside. In a heartbeat, an idea came to her—crazy maybe, but it might work.

Kasey scanned the scaffolding and spotted what she needed: a jagged edge of metal sticking out dangerously. With only the briefest hesitation because she knew her dad was gonna be pretty pissed, she used the sharp metal to slash a tear in the seam of her jacket. Holding the coat to the metal with one hand, she jerked hard, ripping the sleeve wide open. Kasey ran her hands through her hair, messing it up as much as she could. She hit record on the camera and took off running for the garage door.

"Help!" Kasey screamed, waving her arms in panic. The truck had just started rolling again, but jolted to a stop. "Please, somebody, help me!"

She ran past the startled truck driver and into the warehouse. Kasey stopped in the center of the cavernous space. She spun around as if looking for someone to come to her rescue, but she was actually sweeping the camera in every direction to film as much as she could. The driver jumped out of his vehicle and several workers hurried toward her.

Three men surrounded her, all with East Asian features. One of them was older and seemed to be in charge. "You must leave this place," he said. But he seemed to believe her act, not at all worried that a thirteen-year-old girl might pose a threat.

"This weird man," Kasey cried. "He was following me and then he grabbed my arm and I just ran." Kasey glanced all around the warehouse, hoping for some indication that Ryan's mom might be here. Except for a small office, though, it was one huge open space. Lots of boxes and equipment around, but there was no obvious place to hide a hostage.

"You must go!"

"What if he's still out there?" Kasey knew she was almost out of time, keeping the camera hidden in her palm as she tried to film behind her.

The man finally noticed the awkward motions she was making with her hand. He stepped toward her threateningly, reaching for her hand.

"Watch it!" Kasey snapped, stepping back.

But the man had seen the camera and he grabbed for it once more. Kasey dodged, running for the garage door. The truck driver grabbed her as she passed, but he only caught the torn sleeve. It ripped the rest of the way, coming off completely in his hand!

Kasey dashed out the garage door as the men yelled behind her. She never looked back as she raced toward Danny. "Go! *Go!*"

Danny jumped from his hiding place and ran with her around the block. "I told you it was a terrible idea," he said.

Four blocks and several turns later, they finally slowed down, checking behind them. Breathing heavily, Kasey said, "I think we lost them." She leaned against the wall, her hands and legs shaking. That was the scariest, stupidest, best thing she'd ever done in her life!

"Oh my god, you're as crazy as Ryan," Danny wheezed.

Kasey handed him the camera. "I filmed the whole place, I think. But Ryan's mom isn't there. The warehouse doesn't have any rooms to hide her in."

Danny was disappointed. "There're still two other properties to check. Think we should take a look?"

"Definitely," Kasey said. "But it'll have to wait until after school. First bell's in six minutes and I can't afford a tardy. My dad's already gonna be mad enough I ruined my new coat."

Danny smiled. "Really? You bust into a building filled with guys who might shoot you on sight, run for your life through the streets of New York—and you're worried about a *tardy*?"

CHAPTER
30

**NANSANG PROVINCE,
ANDAKAR**

Gunshots echoed through the night as Ryan fought his way up the hillside. After changing back into his high-tops, T-shirt, and jeans, Ryan had started along the perilous path. The jungle's thick undergrowth made the climb difficult, but Ryan forced himself to keep moving forward. He had been on the run for what seemed like hours and had actually come to look forward to the occasional gunshots. Every time he heard another shot it gave him hope. If the ASI soldiers were still firing, they probably hadn't caught Tasha.

Not much moonlight penetrated the canopy of leaves overhead and, twice already, he had nearly twisted his ankle when he failed to see an obstacle hidden in the shadows. But this wasn't Ryan's first time trekking at night. Over the years, his family had been on camping trips to all sorts of crazy spots: on a camel trek in the Sahara desert, at the top of a volcano in Ecuador, and in the shadow of Mount Everest in Nepal.

During every trip, they would take a "Moon Hike," where no flashlights or lanterns were allowed. As a kid, he'd been scared of the dark and always dreaded these excursions. But when he was eight, they took a trip to Iceland and camped by a series of towering waterfalls. His mom took him out on the "Moon Hike" that night, and they trekked up the falls. At the top, Ryan was shocked to discover the sky was lit up with a cascade of violet and green pulsing lights. It was his first glimpse of the northern lights, the most beautiful thing he'd ever seen. It was also the last time Ryan was afraid of the dark.

Scrambling over a fallen tree, Ryan stopped for a moment, looking back. There was no sign of pursuit, so he took a moment to sit and catch his breath. He pulled out his phone and turned it on, but couldn't get a signal.

During the difficult climb, Ryan had dumped

everything from his knapsack other than food. All that was left was one last piece of fruit, a red mangosteen. He tore it open to reveal the white pulp inside and ate every juicy bite. Getting to his feet, Ryan folded the bag and stuck it in his pocket in case he needed it later.

The steep path got increasingly challenging and for the next ten minutes Ryan struggled. It ended at a vertical outcropping of rock, and Ryan had to find a foothold in order to lift himself high enough to grab the upper edge. Physically exhausted and emotionally drained, it took all the strength he had to haul himself up and over the ledge.

But Ryan was surprised and excited to discover that he'd finally made it to the top. Breathing heavily, he looked out across the plateau before him. Misty fog and silvery moonlight gave everything an eerie glow. Ancient stone temples were scattered across the field, their whitewashed domes pale against the night sky. The villager had told him these were the Mae Wong Temples, a Buddhist stronghold abandoned long ago. Ryan wondered if his father had made it this far.

The man had directed John Quinn to a secret chamber located inside a temple with a gold-plated dome. That was the first place Ryan wanted to check, and he headed directly to the closest of the temples. But in the moonlight, it was hard to tell which domes were gold and which were regular stone.

Ryan was so preoccupied with searching for the right temple that he almost missed the ASI soldier patrolling fewer than fifty yards ahead of him. Just as the soldier turned, Ryan saw him. He dropped to the ground, not moving a muscle. Ryan held his breath for what seemed like forever. Finally, the soldier moved on, passing behind one of the pagodas.

Keeping silent, Ryan raced across the open ground and pressed against another of the numerous temples. Peering around the corner, he saw a second soldier pass in the distance. When the sentry wandered out of sight, Ryan darted toward the next pagoda, using it to shield him from view. Through the fog, he caught a glimmer of light shining off one of the domes, taller than the others. Could that be the gold temple the villager described?

Hearing a shout from behind, Ryan whirled around, just in time to see a soldier raise his rifle and fire. Ryan dodged around the side of the temple as the bullet shattered the stone where he'd been standing.

Ryan sprinted away, zigzagging so he didn't make an easy target. Another shot rang out, this one from the second sentry. They were cornering him from two directions. His best chance to stay alive was to take out these two before they could radio for help—and pray there weren't even more of them lurking in the shadows.

Darting around another building so he couldn't be seen, Ryan abruptly stopped, crouching, waiting silently. The two soldiers yelled to one another as they gave chase, attempting to cut Ryan off and trap him between them. But as the first soldier came around the corner, Ryan swung around and smashed his foot, heel first, into the man's right knee! The soldier screamed in pain as he tumbled to the ground, dropping his rifle. Ryan was pretty sure the kick had broken his leg.

Ryan grabbed the weapon, only to see the soldier wasn't giving up. He had pulled a handgun from its holster. Ryan smashed the butt end of the rifle at him, obliterating the man's nose and knocking him out cold.

Hearing boots approach from the other direction, Ryan pressed his advantage. Instead of running, he dropped the rifle and charged forward, meeting the second soldier just as he rounded the corner. Using his smaller size to his advantage, Ryan grabbed the man around the waist and lifted him straight up. The soldier flipped over Ryan's shoulder, landing on his back with a thud. As he struggled to sit, Ryan delivered a perfect Krav Maga chop to his neck, striking the vagus nerve and rendering him instantly unconscious. The guy dropped back to the ground. He'd be out of it for a while, and when he did wake up, he'd have a heck of a headache.

Ryan turned, only to discover he was staring down the barrel of a rifle. Another soldier! Ryan knew there was no getting away this time. It was over. There was no one left to help his parents now.

But as the person holding the rifle stepped out of the shadows and into the moonlight, Ryan saw it wasn't another soldier, after all. It was a girl, probably only a few years older than him.

The rifle never wavered as her finger hovered over the trigger. She said something to him in Andalese, her tone fierce and accusatory.

Ryan raised his hands in surrender. "I'm sorry. I don't understand."

Her expression changed, confusion replacing suspicion. "Who are you?" she asked, in perfect English.

Ryan's instinct told him that the truth was the only thing that might save him. "My name is Ryan. I'm looking for my father, John Quinn. He came to your country to help Myat Kaw."

She slowly lowered her rifle and looked him right in the eye.

"My name is Lan," she said. "I am Myat Kaw."

PART THREE

NO WAY OUT

CHAPTER
31

**MOUNT BANA,
ANDAKAR**

Lan never intended to become a rebel.

Two years ago, she was just a normal schoolgirl. Well, maybe not normal exactly. Lan's life in Andakar was more comfortable than most kids. She knew that now.

Lan's father was a lawyer with the Ministry of Justice, which meant the family was part of the government's inner circle. That came with a lot of perks: a nice house, plenty to eat, and people to help with the cooking and cleaning. She had good friends and went to a school that was only for the children of Andakar's government workers. If it weren't for her father, Lan would never have even questioned how easy they had it.

But Lan's dad didn't allow her to simply

accept the comfortable life they led. He worked inside the system, but insisted it was only so that he could help change it. He represented the citizens of Andakar in the government's courts where they didn't stand a chance of being treated fairly. Lan's father would fight for them even though he knew it was usually pointless. Occasionally, he would win some small victory. On those rare days, he would be filled with passion, insisting that change would come to Andakar, but that it moved as slowly as the sluggish Chin Yon River.

Back then, Lan was impatient with her father's lectures. She was fourteen—she was interested in her friends and music and boys. What happened outside her comfortable world didn't seem to matter that much.

But everything changed after the car crash.

A freak accident, they told her. Both her parents killed instantly. She could barely function. Nothing made sense.

And then her uncle showed up. Aung Win was her father's brother, but the two had grown distant. Lan had not even seen him in over a year. She had always been a little afraid of her uncle. He watched everything with suspicion and disapproval. She didn't know much about him, really. Only that he was high up in the government and had no other family. He disagreed strongly with her father's belief that the people of Andakar should be given more freedom and real justice. The brothers argued about it whenever they were together.

When Aung Win told her that she would be coming to live with him in Panai, she didn't understand at first. She wouldn't leave her friends, her school, everything she'd ever known. Her uncle tried to be comforting, but she could tell he was annoyed by her protests. In the end, she had no choice. It had already been decided. There was nothing she could do about it.

Lan soon learned that her uncle was a general with Andakar's feared secret police, the Army Services Intelligence agency. Her new home was a penthouse on the top floor of the Kali Thawar Hotel. The old hotel was now ASI headquarters, its lower floors housing the strategic command center. The suites on the upper floors had been modernized and now provided luxurious apartments for the ASI's top officers.

From the beginning, Lan and Aung Win had problems. No other kids lived at the Kali Thawar. Lan felt isolated and depressed, lost in this new and unfamiliar place. Her uncle was gone most of the time, leaving her with a caretaker and a teacher who would come to their suite. She was virtually a prisoner in the old hotel.

Eventually, bored and restless, she snuck into her uncle's study—which was, of course, strictly off-limits—and began to explore. This was her first hint of the horrors that her uncle oversaw in his role as the head of the Internal Security Division. From what she could tell, Aung Win's job was to spy on the citizens of Andakar and to arrest anyone suspected of working against the military rulers. She discovered photos of torture that made her run to the bathroom and vomit.

Lan realized she was living among monsters. Not just Aung Win, but the entire ASI and the government itself. She finally understood how sheltered her life had been and how tough it was for most people in her country. She thought often of her father's lectures—how she wished she could hear him go on and on about justice and freedom just one more time! She needed a reason to move on, a purpose. And now she had one.

Inside the walls of the ASI, Lan had access to the country's most closely guarded secrets. All of the ASI soldiers were men, and no one thought anything of the quiet teenage girl who was always around. It took months of watching her uncle and winning his trust, but she gradually discovered the password to his computer and learned the inner workings of the command center downstairs. Piece by piece, Lan gathered intelligence. She taught herself how to get past the security firewalls on the internet that kept Andakar's citizens cut off from the rest of the world. She would use the hated spy agency's own resources against it.

As a child, Lan loved a bedtime story her father told of the monkey and the tiger. The two met in the jungle one day. The tiger put its giant paw on the monkey's tail, pinning it down. The tiger roared and prepared to take a deadly bite. The monkey knew it was hopeless—the tiger was so much bigger than she was—but she didn't give up. Instead, she dug down deep and roared right back at the tiger! The tiger had never been roared at before and was quite surprised. For just a moment, he let go of the monkey's tail. In a flash, the monkey ran away and climbed high into the trees. Lan loved to hear her father do the monkey's roar. The little monkey's name was Myat Kaw.

Using the alias Myat Kaw, Lan began to release the secrets she had uncovered. She learned to hide her tracks and watched in disbelief as the information slowly made its way around the world, outraging the public. For months, she had been exposing the corruption at the heart of Andakar's military rulers. She never set out to be a rebel, but that's what they called her.

Lan realized it couldn't last forever. Her uncle was leading the hunt to find Myat Kaw, so she was able to follow the investigation. They were getting close: tracing the blog posts, breaking through her cyber defenses, cracking down on anyone suspected of supporting Myat Kaw. She knew she'd have to leave soon and made plans to escape.

But she'd waited too long.

Five days ago, Lan had entered the large apartment she shared with her uncle to find Aung Win waiting. He was furious, but his anger was cold and quiet.

"You made a mistake," he told her.

Lan's survival instincts had kicked in. She instantly adopted a passive, confused expression. What was he talking about?

Aung Win showed her a report he'd received on a dissident they'd arrested several days ago. The ASI techs had analyzed his computer and found a communication between the man and someone inside the Kali Thawar. Aung Win admitted he had become suspicious of Lan and the way she had watched his movements all the time, thinking he didn't notice. But he couldn't believe his niece was really capable of betraying him like this.

He had used the dissident's computer to set a trap. He sent an email with a tracking program expertly hidden in the data. And a response had just been received from one of the offices on the second floor. Aung Win held up a tablet that showed surveillance footage of the office: Lan was right there, sitting at the desk using the computer in a room she had no reason to be in.

Aung Win's anger erupted violently then. He had taken her in when no one would! He was the only family she had! How could she do this to him?

But over the past year, Lan had become an excellent liar. She pretended she had no idea what he was talking about, insisting she would never do anything to hurt him after all he'd done for her. It killed her to say those words, but she knew she was fighting for her life.

Aung Win wasn't convinced, but her forceful denials surprised him. He got called away, promising they would finish this when he returned. She would tell him the truth, one way or another. He locked her into her room when he left.

Which was just what Lan wanted. She had a rope stashed outside her window and used it to slide all the way down to the ground. Months of sneaking around the Kali Thawar command center had prepared her for an escape. Within minutes, she made it out of the compound and into the streets of Panai.

If not for John Quinn, she was sure the ASI would have found her within hours—they had eyes everywhere. The American had rescued her, but he'd paid a terrible price.

Now, his son stood in front of her, waiting anxiously for the answer to the question he had just asked.

"Yes," she told him. "Your father's alive."

CHAPTER
32

**MOUNT BANA,
ANDAKAR**

Ryan tied the hands of one unconscious soldier as Lan bound the feet of the other. His head was swimming with the quick download of information she had given him.

"Shot?" he repeated. "How bad? Is he okay?"

"He's getting better. It went straight through his leg."

"Where is he? Take me to him."

"He needs water," Lan said. "We both do. Help me get supplies, then we'll go."

Ryan didn't want to wait another second. "I want to see him now."

But Lan was adamant. "He's feverish and fighting infection. We ran out of medicine and water yesterday. We need to grab whatever we can find before more soldiers show up."

Frustrated, Ryan wanted to argue but knew she was right. "Fine—let's just hurry."

"Are you out here by yourself?" she asked, dragging one of the soldiers out of sight.

"Why?" Ryan grabbed the other one by the ankles and pulled.

"You just seem young, that's all."

"You're one to talk. You've been single-handedly taking on the entire government." Ryan was still having trouble believing this teen-age girl was the notorious Myat Kaw. Lan wasn't at all what he expected. She actually looked rather delicate, short and thin with a round face, high cheekbones, and black hair pulled back into a ponytail. But her eyes betrayed the feroc-ity of a survivor. This girl was a fighter.

"We need to find their jeep," Lan said, scan-ning the area. She led the way, cautiously check-ing around the corner of every temple before moving forward.

"How'd you get hooked up with my dad?" Ryan asked. Lan glanced over, and Ryan could tell she was debating how much to tell him. "I think you can trust me—my dad got *shot* for you."

"Sorry. It's been hard to trust anyone the last few months." Lan kept moving as she spoke, trying to locate the jeep. "A few weeks ago, things started getting really bad. The ASI was coming after me with everything they had. I knew, eventually, they'd find out who I was. I needed a way out of Andakar. Some supporters put me in touch with this group that helps people like me out of bad situations."

Ryan nodded. "The ERC."

"John Quinn contacted me and offered to help. But I thought we still had time. A few days ago, everything went wrong and I had to run. I got word to your dad and then hid out until he could get here." Lan suddenly pointed. "There!"

The jeep was parked under the outstretched boughs of a banyan tree. They watched from behind a stone wall for a few moments, making sure no one else was around, then moved forward.

"I'll take the back," Ryan said. As they searched the jeep, opening bags and searching compartments, he asked, "How did my dad get shot?"

"The ASI agents were always close behind. I think someone in Thanlin must be an informer for them because they were on us almost immediately. We had just made it to the temple grounds when the bullet hit your father. I thought we were dead."

Ryan stopped searching, looking at her. "What happened?"

"Your dad's stubborn. He yelled at me, and I finally snapped out of it." Ryan remembered plenty of times his dad had pushed him in the same way. Lan continued, "We barely made it to the temple. John was about to pass out by that point. And then I couldn't find the secret entrance the guide told us about. I could hear more soldiers arriving, shouting. They were so close."

Reliving it, she lapsed into silence. Ryan prodded her, "But you made it."

"Yeah. I dragged him inside and we were finally safe. We had a first-aid kit and medicine in our packs, so I patched him up the best I could. I've given him all the antibiotics. His fever has come down a lot since yesterday." She held up two canteens. "Water."

Ryan realized that she had probably saved his father's life. Of course, his dad would've never been here in the first place if not for her.

He unzipped a canvas bag, dumping out the ammunition inside. "Here—we can carry everything in this."

Lan tossed him the canteens and a flashlight she pulled out of the glove compartment. "I don't think the ASI knows he got shot. The area was crawling with soldiers that night and all the next day. They searched everywhere, but then they all left except for the two we tied up. The rest moved on toward the border. They must think we got away."

The squawk from a radio startled them both. Lan found it wedged between the front seats, the size of a brick with an antenna sticking out the top. She listened to two voices communicating for a moment, then translated for Ryan. "We're okay for now. They're searching on the far side of Mount Bana."

Ryan felt his stomach clench. "Did they say anything about capturing anyone?"

"No."

So there was still hope for Tasha. Ryan found a box filled with rations, cans of meat and individual meal bars, and dumped the whole thing into the bag. Lan clipped the soldiers' radio to her pants as Ryan zipped the canvas bag, slinging it over his shoulder. "Let's go."

Their raid complete, Ryan and Lan made their way to the temple with the golden dome. Its walls were covered with elaborate depictions of scenes from the life of the Buddha. Vines covered much of the surface, wrapping across the stone like serpents consuming the ancient structure. Lan ducked into the pitch-black entrance without hesitation, swallowed by the shadows.

With its ghostly emptiness and the buzz of jungle insects echoing all around, the place gave Ryan the creeps, but he fought his anxiety and followed.

Inside, shafts of moonlight lit the temple with a pale glow. He was in a huge room, the ground littered with debris. Lan stood in front of a massive, solid wall.

"Help me. It's heavy."

Confused, Ryan approached. A sculpture of a man and woman, palms pressed together in prayer, was carved into the stone. They were kneeling on some kind of raised altar engraved with intricate symbols. Lan put both hands on the edge of the altar as if to push it.

"It's a solid wall," Ryan said.

"That's exactly what the king's guard believed when they came to slaughter the monks that lived here five hundred years ago. They were wrong." With a grimace, Lan pushed on the altar and, to Ryan's amazement, it moved. She looked back. "You just gonna stand there?"

Ryan joined her and, together, they pushed. The sculpture was heavy but had been engineered to move smoothly. It pivoted on its axis, revealing a dimly lit tunnel just beyond. When it was wide enough, they slipped through the opening, and then pushed the stone back into place.

The tunnel wasn't long but it led to a hollowed-out chamber. A battery-powered lantern gave enough light for Ryan to see the crumpled form of his father resting against the far wall.

John Quinn raised his head, looking up in utter disbelief. "Ryan . . . ?"

"Hey, Dad. You're not an easy guy to find."

CHAPTER
33

**MOUNT BANA,
ANDAKAR**

Seeing his father again, Ryan remembered a time when he must have been around five years old. His dad was about to leave on another of his many trips and Ryan begged him not to go. It was the third time in a month he'd left. When Ryan was little, he had always missed his dad to the point of tears.

John had pulled his son up into his arms and held him close. He smelled like he'd just shaved. "I know it's hard to be apart," his father told him. "But the work I do, it's important. It makes a difference in people's lives."

"I don't care," Ryan had insisted. "I just want you here."

"You might not care now. But one day, I hope

you will. You know how much I love you, right?"

Begrudgingly, Ryan had nodded.

"And I always come back, don't I? No one in the world is more important to me than you and your mother. So give me a kiss, and we'll be back together before you know it."

Now, Ryan sat next to his dad on the hard, stone floor of the temple. John's leg was bloody and bandaged, his face filthy. Was this what those trips had always been like? How many times had Ryan come this close to losing his father and never even known it?

"The leg's healing. It's just taking time." John was doing his best to convince Ryan he felt better than he looked.

"You need a hospital," Ryan said.

"I'll be okay. Another couple of days of rest and I can travel." John took a long drink from one of the canteens. "You shouldn't be here."

Ryan was confused—it sounded like his dad was mad at him. "You shouldn't be, either." Across the chamber, Lan ate quietly, trying to give them privacy. But in this small room, Ryan knew she could hear every word.

"Where's Mom?" Dad asked.

"I don't know."

"She's not with you?"

Ryan lowered his voice. "She's been kid-napped. Because of *this*. Because of her."

"What?" John's tone was sharp, not caring that Lan could hear them. "What happened?"

"These guys were following me. Then, they came to the house. I tried to fight them off, but . . . I wasn't good enough. They took Mom. They were from Andakar—the one in charge is called Aung Win."

"Aung Win is in New York?"

"He was a couple of days ago. You know him?"

But it was Lan who answered. "Aung Win is my uncle. He's a general in the ASI."

Ryan's dad was confused. "He targeted my family, which means he knows who I am. How could he have identified me? We were careful."

"I did exactly what you told me," Lan said. "I only used that private chat room you set up, and I never wrote anything down."

"No one's blaming you." John turned to Ryan. "Is Mom okay? Have you talked to her?"

"She was when I left. It's why I came." Ryan glanced at Lan, not sure how to continue with her standing right there. Lan understood and moved away, sitting back down against the wall.

"Aung Win wants to trade," Ryan whispered.

"Mom for her. He said we have five days. That's three days from now."

"That's not going to happen," John said. He tried to stand before Ryan could stop him. "We have to get home."

"Dad, stop—"

John faltered, grabbing his leg, grimacing in pain. Ryan helped him back down as Lan came over, opening a bottle of pain pills from the medical kit. "Give him these. They're the last two."

Ryan helped his father take the pills and sip some water. "We'll figure it out, Dad. Mom's gonna be okay." He said the words but didn't really believe them.

For several minutes, John leaned his head back against the wall, eyes closed. When he opened them, he looked at Ryan. "You must have a lot of questions."

"You think?" Ryan was glad to see his dad smile. For a brief moment, it felt almost normal.

"But I have one first," John said. "How did you even get here?"

"It wasn't that hard. I just used my new credit card. The one I found with my fake passport in the secret room behind the wall of your study." Ryan couldn't keep the bitterness out of his voice. "And then I tagged along with this really obnoxious woman who showed up on a motor-cycle. Turns out, she knew more about my parents than I did."

John's expression clouded. "Wait—are you talking about Tasha Levi?"

"Yeah. We got separated."

"Why is Tasha here?"

"She's trying to help me find *you*. Which may have gotten her captured or killed!" Ryan knew he must be exhausted because it was hard to keep his emotions in check. Now that he was with his dad, part of him just wanted to let go and be a kid. To throw a tantrum or even cry, which he almost never did. Instead, he asked, "When were you gonna tell me about the ERC?"

"When you were ready."

"You didn't think I could handle the truth?"

"Mom and I wanted you to have a normal life. We've been training you practically since you were born. But you needed to be old enough to make your own decisions before you chose whether to get involved or not."

"I don't want to be involved. And I don't want you to be, either. I just want to go back to our regular lives and forget all this." Ryan could see the disappointment in his father's eyes, but he didn't care. He'd believed if he could just find his dad, then everything would be all right. John Quinn would figure out what to do. He always had.

But looking at him now, Ryan knew his father wasn't in any condition to fix this situation. Not in time to help Mom. Only three days were left before Aung Win carried out his threat to kill her if he didn't get Myat Kaw. And it would take a whole day just to fly back to New York.

Which meant that time was running out fast.

Ryan and Lan locked eyes across the room. He had the feeling she could tell exactly what he was thinking: *He'd make whatever sacrifice was necessary if it meant saving his mom.*

CHAPTER
34

**NEW YORK,
USA**

anny and Kasey met after school, sitting close together on a courtyard bench so they could share Danny's computer. He had uploaded the video recording Kasey shot of the warehouse, making it easier to see on the bigger screen.

"What *is* all that stuff?" Kasey asked, pointing to the boxes stacked all around. "I know they weren't hiding Ryan's mom there, but they sure seemed like they were being secretive about something."

Danny highlighted the area of the screen with the boxes and hit a couple of keys. The image enlarged so they could see the side of one of the boxes, which was labeled: LTV Technologies. Danny Googled the company. "Looks like LTV does a lot of work with the US military. Wow—missile-guidance systems, lasers—this is super-high-tech."

"The United States would never let LTV sell that kind of stuff to a dictatorship like Andakar. It's too dangerous."

"Which means they're probably stealing the technology, then shipping it back to Andakar secretly." Danny fast-forwarded the video to another section showing a small forklift moving a stack of crates. "Yeah, see there? Those crates are marked with a Red Cross logo. I bet that's how they get it all out of the country."

Kasey was excited. "We could use this with the police. I bet this is enough for them to arrest those guys. Maybe they can force them to tell where Ryan's mom is?"

"But what if they don't know? Or what if this Aung Win finds out the police are asking questions and just kills her?"

Kasey wasn't ready to give up on her idea, though. "He could do that anyway. We can tell them they have to be careful."

Danny thought about it and finally nodded. "Maybe you're right. But let me email Ryan first. Make sure he's cool with it."

"Deal."

As Danny typed the email, Kasey stood. "But we're still checking out that other address tonight, right?"

"Will you be able to sneak out?" Danny asked.

"I think so. My dad's got some event, so it's just me and my brothers. I'll tell them I'm crashing early and close my door." Kasey seemed unsure, admitting: "I've never snuck out before."

Danny nodded. "Me, neither. My mom'll ground me for a year if she finds out."

"Then maybe you'd better not do it." Danny and Kasey both jumped at the voice behind them. The African American woman was tall and imposing, dressed in a dark blue suit and wearing sunglasses. "Sneaking out can lead to all kinds of trouble."

Kasey recovered first, facing the woman. "It's really rude to eavesdrop on people."

"But you hear such interesting things." The woman smiled, taking off her sunglasses and staring at Danny. "You're Danny Santiago?"

"Nope. Never heard of him." Danny stuffed his laptop into his bag and stood next to Kasey.

"Danny, my name is Agent Calloway." The woman flashed her credentials, revealing the bald-eagle logo of the Central Intelligence

Agency. "I'm concerned for a friend of yours."

"For Kasey?" Danny widened his eyes in mock surprise. "Kasey's fine—aren't you, Kasey?"

Agent Calloway smiled, but she wasn't at all amused. "You know who I mean. Ryan Quinn. He may be in trouble, and I'd like to help."

Before Danny could deny it, Kasey cut him off. "What do you know about Ryan?"

The agent turned her cool gaze on Kasey. "I know that he hasn't been seen since Monday evening. Neither has his mother. And his father's been associating with some bad men. I'm afraid that somehow Ryan and his mom got caught in the middle."

"Wait," Kasey said. "You think Ryan's dad is some kind of criminal?"

"I'm not sure. That's why we want to talk to him. But maybe you know something about him that I don't?"

"He's a hero, not a criminal—"

Before she could say anything more, Danny jumped in. "That's right—a *hero* to all of us kids who like to hang out at their house—and order pizza and sodas!" Both Kasey and Agent Calloway were perplexed by Danny's outburst. "Because John Quinn orders great pizza! And buys tons of soda. To drink. Which is totally heroic."

Agent Calloway regarded the two of them. "Your friend could be in danger. You sure there's nothing you'd like to tell me?"

"Ryan's just sick," Danny said, with a warning look at Kasey. "But if we hear from him, we'll tell him you're looking."

Agent Calloway pulled business cards from her suit pocket. "You do that. Here's my number." She gave a card to each of them. "I really do just want to help."

She stared at them each a moment more, letting her words sink in, then moved off. When she was out of earshot, Kasey turned to Danny. "Why do they think Ryan's dad is a criminal?"

"Ryan said they had some pictures of Mr. Quinn with this notorious smuggler in Thailand. He was probably paying the guy to smuggle him into Andakar, but they don't know that."

"So let's tell them. I mean, what are we doing? This is crazy—we're being questioned by the *CIA*! If they know the truth, maybe they'll help him."

"We can't, Kasey." Danny suddenly realized he might have made a mistake getting Kasey involved. She had a point—this was out of hand, and now he'd made her a part of it.

"Why not?"

"Because what they do—this whole Emergency Rescue Committee thing—it *is* illegal. They use fake passports to sneak into countries. Probably bribe officials and hack into government records. Sneak across borders. Who knows what else? They could get arrested for any of those things."

"That's stupid—they're *helping* people," Kasey insisted.

"I know. And they could pay a terrible price for it if we're not careful." Danny understood her frustration. "Look, don't worry about checking out that building tonight. I'll probably just blow it off anyway."

"No, you won't," Kasey said. "You're just saying that because you think I'm freaking out. And I guess I am a little."

"It's a completely justified freak-out."

"Hey, Kasey!" They both turned to see Drew Stieglitz, Kasey's brother. "Come on, let's go!"

Kasey grabbed her backpack. "If I can get out, maybe I'll see you tonight."

"You don't need to," Danny said, and he meant it.

"Text me if anything changes." She took off, running to join her brother. Steeg glared at Danny like he wanted to rip his head off. Danny smirked and waved, just pissing off the muscular jock even more.

And that gave Danny the only smile he'd had all day.

CHAPTER
35

**MOUNT BANA,
ANDAKAR**

Wake up. They're coming."

Ryan turned over as Lan shook him. He was groggy and his body ached from sleeping a few hours on the stone floor. But the alarm in Lan's expression snapped him into focus.

"Soldiers?"

Lan held up the radio they had taken from the jeep. "I had to go outside to get a signal. But I heard them talking. The two guards we tied up didn't report in, so they're sending a squad."

Ryan realized that Lan was whispering. She also had her backpack on. "What are you doing?"

"Making a run for it before they get here."

"That's crazy. We'll stay here—they didn't find you before."

"That's only because they thought we'd escaped. That we were heading to the border. I know the ASI. If they think there's a chance we're here somewhere, they'll burn all the temples to the ground." She looked over at John, who was still sleeping. "And your father can't travel yet. He needs at least another day or two."

Ryan knew she was right, but he still didn't understand her plan. "So what're you gonna do?"

"Lead them away," Lan said. "I'll make sure they see me. If they follow me, then they'll leave you and John alone. They won't even know you're here."

"They'll kill you."

"Maybe. I just don't want them to catch me. That would be much worse." Lan stood and Ryan got up, going after her.

"Don't do this—we can all wait it out together."

"I made the choice to become Myat Kaw, not you or your father. I'll deal with it." She turned back. "Tell your dad *thanks*."

Ryan didn't know what to do as she disappeared into the tunnel that led to the exit. This was suicide. Or worse—he'd seen the kind of torture the ASI used. What would they do to someone who had spilled all their most-guarded secrets? Ryan didn't even want to imagine.

This wasn't his problem. So why did he feel responsible? He'd just met this girl! But it didn't seem right. She'd been so brave, standing up to these tyrants and risking everything. And now they were probably gonna catch her and make her suffer and—

Ryan reacted without thinking. He grabbed his own bag, stuffing a flashlight and a couple of the meal bars inside. He heard the grinding of the stone moving at the entrance as he closed the bag and slung it over his shoulder.

"What's going on?" Ryan turned to find his dad sitting up. "Where's Lan?"

"The ASI's coming. We're gonna lead them away from here."

"No, you're not!" John tried to stand, but Ryan went to him. He put a hand on his dad's shoulder, keeping him from rising.

"I am, Dad. Lan's already gone and I can't let her try to do it on her own. She's got a better chance if I'm there to help."

"It's too dangerous—you're not ready."

"I found you, didn't I? I got here on my own, and, somehow, I'm gonna get Lan out of Andakar. Besides, what choice do we have? If the ASI catches Lan, what do you think Aung Win will do with Mom? You think he's really gonna just let her go?"

John wanted to argue, but Ryan could tell that he agreed. Once Aung Win had what he wanted, he'd make sure there was no one left alive who could reveal what had happened. They had to keep Lan safe, not just for her own sake, but for Jacqueline's.

"Get my bag," John barked.

John sat against the wall as Ryan grabbed the pack and handed it to him. John dug inside, pulling out a passport, some Baggies, and a roll of fabric tape. "This is Lan's passport. It's fake, but it's top-quality. It'll get her across the border into Thailand."

"Okay," Ryan said, about to put it in his bag.

"No." His dad stopped him. "Always keep everything important wrapped up tight and taped to your body. Passports, cell phone, emergency money."

Ryan nodded, glancing toward the exit. "I have to go."

John held his arm tight. "You need to make your way down the mountain to the town of Hodaw. You should get cell reception once you cross to the other side of Mount Bana. Memorize this number." John spouted out a ten-digit number.

"Why?"

"Just do it." John was all business, giving Ryan the sense of what he must be like on a mission. He said the number once more, then made Ryan repeat it.

"Tell the man who answers to initiate the extraction out of Hodaw. His name is Simon McClelland. He'll tell you what to do next."

"Is he the smuggler?" Ryan asked, remembering the CIA's questions.

John was obviously surprised Ryan knew, but didn't waste time on it. "You can trust Simon. I helped him out of a bad situation once."

Ryan stood. He had to go now or risk losing Lan. "There's enough food and water here for a week. Will you be okay?"

"Don't worry about me. I'll follow as soon as I can put pressure on my leg. When Aung Win calls, try to stall him. See if you can buy us a couple of more days so I can deal with him."

"I'll try." Ryan headed for the tunnel.

"Ryan." Worry and fear were etched across his dad's face. "Be careful. You know how much I love you, right?"

Ryan remembered his father's same words all those years ago when he was a boy. He tried his best to offer the reassurance his dad had once given him: "We'll be together again before you know it."

But neither one of them seemed convinced that was the truth.

CHAPTER 36

**MOUNT BANA,
ANDAKAR**

They had been traveling since just before dawn. As the temperature rose, the sun finally burned off the morning fog. This side of the mountain was rockier, the descent slippery and treacherous. Lan had boots, but Ryan's high-tops sucked for this kind of climbing, and they still had another four hours of trekking ahead.

They didn't talk much, hiking together in silence. Lan had pretended to be upset when Ryan joined her, but he was pretty sure she was secretly relieved. As they left the temple grounds, they made sure the tied-up guards saw which direction they headed. They needed the squad to follow them so Ryan's dad would be safe.

Lan had the soldiers' radio turned low. "I'm sorry about what's happening," she said. "It's my fault your mother and father are in danger."

"No, it's not. They chose this kind of life. I think danger comes with the territory."

"Sounds like you don't approve."

"I just want a normal life. Getting chased by soldiers with machine guns is definitely *not* normal." As they continued along the rocky path, Ryan realized he knew almost nothing about Lan. There was undoubtedly a lot more to her than her blog posts. "Where are your parents?" he asked.

"They died. A car crash." Lan kept walking, not looking at him.

"That's terrible. I'm sorry." Ryan didn't know what else to say. Maybe he should've just kept his mouth shut.

After a few steps, Lan spoke. "I think the idea of a 'normal' life is a lie. It was for me, anyway. It's like living inside a bubble. All these horrible things are going on around us, but we just pretend they're not there."

"We can't solve everyone's problems," Ryan said.

"We can't just pretend everything's fine, either."

Ryan had seen a lot in his travels. He knew firsthand how hard some people had it. He had to admire that Lan had actually done something to help. And it had cost her—she was on the run from the only home she'd ever known. He was starting to understand the sacrifice she had made when she became Myat Kaw.

"I think what you did was really brave," he said.

"Brave or stupid." Lan smiled as Ryan offered her a hand, helping her down from a ledge. "I'm still not sure."

"Sometimes brave and stupid aren't that far apart."

Over the next half hour, they talked. She told him about living with Aung Win and how she learned to sneak around the Kali Thawar. He told her about New York City and the kids who went to his school. Lan was fascinated by all the places he'd lived around the world.

"That's what I want to do," she told him. "Travel everywhere. See new things all the time. It sounds great."

"There were a lot of cool things about it, I guess," Ryan admitted. "Definitely better than living with your uncle."

"Anything's better than that. He was so angry when he found out I was Myat Kaw."

Ryan stopped short. "He knows it's you?"

"That's why he's desperate to get me back. He doesn't want his bosses to find out who I am. If they learn Myat Kaw is his niece, they'll know exactly where all that top secret information came from. He'll be ruined. Probably even executed."

They could use that to their advantage, Ryan thought. "Maybe if you agreed not to post anything else, he'd agree to let my mom go? As long as he leaves you alone, you promise not to tell anyone who Myat Kaw really is."

Lan didn't respond, but it was clear she didn't think much of that idea.

"It might work," Ryan added.

"I wish it were that easy. It would be safer for me if the world never found out who I really am. But my uncle won't ever stop. Not if he thinks I pose a threat to him. Eventually, he'll find me."

Ryan knew in his heart she was right. He'd seen Aung Win in action. He was ruthless and not the kind to leave loose ends.

Lan's hand flew to her mouth as she thought of something. "Oh my god . . . the phone."

"What phone?"

"Your dad's." Lan turned to him, looking

horrified. "I've been trying to figure out how my uncle discovered your father was involved. We were always careful—all our messages were encrypted. But the night he was shot, I was so scared. I wasn't thinking straight, just trying to get away. We barely made it to the temple and it was too dark to see. I felt the phone inside his pocket. So I grabbed it and turned it on— just for the light, to be able to find that secret door. When John saw what I'd done, he made me shut it off immediately."

Ryan understood what had happened. "Cell phones can be traced and the number identified. Even when you're not making a call."

"Which means it really *was* my fault. Them finding you, your mom getting taken . . ."

"Don't say that," Ryan said. "You were just trying to survive, doing what—"

"Ryan!" Lan leaped forward, shoving Ryan so hard that both of them tumbled to the ground as—*boom!*—a shot echoed across the mountainside. As they scrambled to their feet, she pointed down the hill. "There!"

Far below, Ryan saw soldiers spreading out across the landscape. They weren't getting past them. Ryan looked uphill instead. "This way!"

Ryan veered toward a thick clump of trees as

more shots rang out. Using the foliage as cover, they ran, jumping rocks and fighting through underbrush. Lan stumbled and hit the ground hard. Ryan ran back, grabbing her hand and forcing her to shake off the pain and keep going.

They made it to the top of a ridge. In the distance, Ryan spotted more military vehicles racing toward their location. As he tried to figure out which way to run, Lan held the radio to her ear, listening closely. "They called for helicopters," she reported.

They couldn't go back down the mountain. But up above, the jagged cliffs appeared impossible to scale. That left no choice but to keep moving around the side of the mountain, the opposite direction from where they wanted to go. Every step was taking them deeper into Andakar and farther from the border with Thailand.

"They're getting closer," Lan warned.

"Let's go." Ryan forged a trail, choosing at every fork to go deeper into the underbrush and, hopefully, make it harder for the soldiers to follow. They might be able to hide if they could put enough distance and obstacles between themselves and the enemy.

After fifteen minutes of relentless running, Lan was out of breath and struggling to keep up. A dull roar became noticeable as they made it through a rough patch of underbrush. "Is that a helicopter?" Lan asked, looking up.

Ryan searched the sky but couldn't see anything. The roar seemed to be coming from all around. Ryan was starting to get a bad feeling about it when he burst through a thick growth of trees and into a clearing. He came to an immediate halt, not believing what he was seeing.

"They're catching up," Lan said as she crashed through the underbrush. She rushed into the clearing and nearly knocked into Ryan.

Lan froze, seeing what Ryan was staring at: Ten feet ahead, the ground abruptly ended in a sheer drop into a deep chasm. The source of the roar became clear. Fifty feet below, a raging river with white-tipped rapids swept its way through the jungle.

They were trapped. There was nowhere left to run.

CHAPTER 37

**MOUNT BANA,
ANDAKAR**

We don't have time for this—we have to run!" Lan glanced nervously back at the trees.

Ryan ignored her. He put the fake passport his dad had given him into a plastic Baggie and sealed it up. "Hold this against your stomach."

Lan was confused, but lifted her shirt and did as Ryan requested. Quickly, he wrapped the fabric tape around her middle, circling her body twice to secure the Baggie. "Do we have to do this now?" she asked impatiently.

"We can't risk losing the passports." Ryan pulled his cell phone from the pocket of his jeans and transported it into another Baggie with his own passport, resealing it quickly. "This phone's supposed to be waterproof, but I'm not risking it."

Lan suddenly understood: "Waterproof?" She looked at the rapids below them. "I'm not a very good swimmer."

"Bet you're better at it than dodging bullets." Ryan taped the Baggie with the passport and phone around his own torso, and then took Lan's hand. He had to practically drag her to the edge of the cliff. Down below, the river snaked along the canyon, cutting through the bamboo and boulders with ferocious power. "When you hit the water, cross your arms over your chest and try to stay on your back. Keep your feet out ahead of you so your boots hit the bottom first. Okay?"

"No, not okay!"

Ryan tried to sound like this was no biggie, but he didn't quite pull it off. "One—two—" Ryan yelled, grabbing her hand once more.

"I can't—" Lan jerked her hand away as a bullet struck the tree just behind them, scattering leaves everywhere.

"THREE!" Ryan yelled and they leaped from the cliff. For a moment, it felt as if they hung suspended in air. Then, both screaming, they plummeted to the water below.

Ryan hit the river at an angle, slicing through the current. He spun around as the water tossed him end over end. Unable to tell which way was up, he struggled to keep his mouth closed. If water got in his lungs, he'd be done. He had to get to the surface.

His shoulder slammed into a boulder, knocking the air out of him. But then he saw bright light above—the sun! The current slowed slightly and Ryan kicked, propelling himself toward the light. He was running out of breath, but he forced himself to keep kicking.

Ryan finally burst to the surface, gasping for air. Paddling hard, he turned himself around so he was facing forward and tried to float on his back. It was nearly impossible—and now he was heading right for a series of rapids.

He tried to slow himself, paddling backward furiously as he looked around for something, anything to slow him down.

"Lan!" he yelled, though it came out more a strangled cry than the shout he was attempting. Ryan felt the first stirring of panic that she might have drowned—

But then Lan popped to the surface ten feet ahead of him! Her arms thrashed in desperation as her head bobbed up and down under the water. She wasn't going to make it, Ryan realized. She'd swallowed a lot of water and would drown unless he did something. "On your back," he yelled, but she either couldn't hear him over the rapids or wasn't paying attention to anything but her own survival.

The next set of rapids was just ahead. Lan needed help. With a surge, Ryan swam toward her, the river's momentum helping him close the distance.

Ryan was going so fast, he practically slammed into her. He grabbed Lan and the look of utter panic in her eyes was all the motivation he needed. Exhaustion creeping in, he spun her around so she faced the sky. "I've got you. Just relax—trust me!"

Ryan pulled her close on top of him and wrapped his arms around her waist. She was small enough that his legs extended beyond her own and, as they hit the next set of rapids, he was able to use his feet to help them navigate the boulders.

They rode the white water, twisting through the curves like they were riding an Olympic toboggan. Ryan's hip slammed into a rock and his head bashed against a branch, but he held her tight. No matter what, he wouldn't let go.

At last, they shot out of the final rapid and into a quieter section of the river. For several seconds, they floated, but Ryan could already feel his feet starting to sink. Not wanting to let Lan go, he held her with one arm while using the other to keep them above the surface.

"You okay?" he asked in a hoarse whisper.

Lan gasped, having difficulty catching her breath. "Fantastic."

Ryan couldn't help but smile. Up ahead, he could see the wide river made a sharp turn. On the side closest to them, an island of rocks and broken bamboo stalks offered the best opportunity to land. He paddled in that direction, but as they approached, the current accelerated.

"Ryan," Lan said, "do you hear that?"

A sound like low, rolling thunder was coming from around the bend. Ryan used his one free arm to stroke even harder, steering them toward the island. Stretching out, Ryan managed to grab hold of a thick bamboo pole, hoping to use it to pull them to safety. But the bamboo wasn't rooted in anything and it wrenched free in his hand.

As they whipped around the bend, the river flowed faster and the lip of a waterfall came into view. Knowing he wouldn't be able to keep hold of Lan against that kind of force, Ryan dragged the bamboo pole under their arms.

"Hold on!" he yelled, as they raced toward the falls.

The bamboo offered just enough resistance to allow them to keep their legs raised high, avoiding the rocks below the surface.

Screaming in unison, they flew over the edge!

CHAPTER
38

**NEW YORK,
USA**

anny glimpsed the shadow of some-one sneaking up behind him just as a hand grabbed his shoulder. Certain he was about to be killed, he screamed, spinning around so fast he lost his balance and fell back-ward, landing on his butt.

But it was only Kasey, who shook her head. "Jumpy much?"

Danny picked himself up, checking to make sure he hadn't damaged his remote control in the fall. He was happy to see her, even if he wasn't going to let her know that. "Get in here before someone sees you!"

Danny stepped aside so Kasey could join him in the alcove where he was hiding. Across from

them was the final address on the list of properties owned by Andakar's government that
Danny had found. It was an old building on this
cobblestone street in SoHo, a trendy section
of New York that had once been nothing but
factories and sweatshops. Though some of the
stores along the block had been updated and
turned into stylish shops, the area maintained
its oppressive, industrial feel.

Danny and Kasey were hidden in the shadows of a stairway that led down to the basement entrance of a bakery. The shop was closed
for the night, so Danny thought it was probably
safe.

"I didn't think you were gonna come," Danny
said.

"My brother was watching me pretty close. I
finally told him I was going to do homework and
go to bed, and just shut my door. Didn't you get
my text?"

"I left my phone at home," Danny explained.
"My mom's out late tonight, but she checks the
GPS on my phone so she always knows where
I am."

"I thought you were this tech genius. Can't
you just disable it?"

"Of *course* I can—give me a little credit. But

sometimes it comes in handy. Like tonight, because she thinks I'm still at the apartment doing my homework."

Kasey noticed the remote control Danny carried. It had a short antenna, two separate joysticks, and a screen right in the middle. "What's that?"

"It's how we're gonna see inside without you doing anything crazy again." From the ground, Danny picked up a remote-control flying drone that had mini helicopter rotors at the end of each appendage. "The XTL Specter with a few Danny Santiago upgrades!"

Underneath the rotors was an electronics rig that housed a tiny camera mounted on a swivel platform. Danny moved the joysticks on his controller and the camera pivoted back and forth. The camera's video feed appeared right on the controller's display screen.

"Your very own spy cam." Kasey looked across the street at the building. "The apartments all look empty. Is anybody even living there?"

"We'll find out. Everything's closed up in the front, and there's no way to get around the sides."

"So what do we do?"

"We go over the top." Danny punched a button on the Specter and the rotor blades started to spin faster and faster, until the drone suddenly lifted straight up. Kasey stepped out of the way as Danny told her, "I made it superquiet—like a stealth drone. Plus, I improved the electronics so it has a five-hundred-yard range and can fly faster than thirty miles an hour."

Eerily silent, the Specter rose above the empty street, zipping sharply from side to side as Danny tested his reflexes with the controls. Kasey looked over his shoulder at the display screen, amazed at the crisp images the camera transmitted.

Danny guided the Specter up the front of the five-story building. All the windows had drapes or blinds pulled across them, and there were no lights on anywhere.

"Weird in New York not to have anybody home," Kasey said.

"I know." Danny manipulated the controls and the drone flew up and over the roof. In back of the building was a private courtyard. He carefully steered the Specter down, allowing it to hover so they could inspect the apartments.

Kasey peered at the screen. The windows back there weren't covered up, but they were still dark. "Go down to the next floor," she said. "I think I see a light." Danny directed the Specter down into the courtyard.

"See?" Kasey pointed. Sure enough, there were lights on inside, but the curtains were drawn, keeping them from seeing much. "Maybe someone's in there, but they don't want anyone to know."

Danny tried to get a better angle, moving the drone in different directions. Suddenly, the curtain jerked aside and a man's face peered out! Danny impulsively pressed both joysticks forward so the Specter rocketed up into the sky.

"It was a guy, but I couldn't see him very well."

"That's okay, I saw him enough for both of us." Danny was urgently guiding the Specter back toward them. "I know who it was."

"You recognized him?"

"It's the same guy who kidnapped Ryan's mom. The big one—the bodyguard."

"We have to call the police."

"We can't. They said no cops." The Specter soared down as Danny brought it in for a landing on the stairway next to their hiding place.

But Kasey was adamant. "Danny, think about it. Ryan's on the other side of the world and his mom may be *right there*. If they're able to save her now, it means this'll all be over."

"But what if they can't? What if she's not there, or something goes wrong and these guys get pissed off?"

"They're the police. They're good at this. A lot better than we are."

Danny knew that Kasey was making sense. He didn't know what to do. He needed to talk to Ryan. "You have your phone, right?" Kasey nodded. "Call Ryan. Maybe we'll get lucky and he'll answer."

Kasey took out her phone and hit a button—Danny noted that she already had Ryan on her Favorites screen—and waited. Please answer, Danny thought, don't make us decide this on our own!

But Kasey shook her head. "Voice mail."

Disappointed, Danny looked at the dark apartment building. "Okay, he finally said. "Let's call the cops."

CHAPTER
39

**LAZU RIVER,
ANDAKAR**

Ryan soared through the air, arms wind-milling uselessly, then plunged into the water. He hit feet first, going deep. The current tugged him forward, and he was somer-saulting underwater—again.

When he finally made it to the surface, Ryan coughed and gasped for air. He scanned the water around him but saw no sign of Lan. The current was slowing, but continued to pull him relentlessly forward. Just ahead, the river they had been traveling along merged with a much larger body of water, wider and slower moving. Ryan finally spotted Lan, clinging to the bamboo pole like a lifeline. She had drifted even farther out into the larger river than Ryan. He swam to her, knowing he needed to calm her before she got more water in her lungs.

"You're okay—take deep breaths," he said, easing her onto her back. The shore was far away in both directions. This river was wider than a football field, and they were dog-paddling right in the middle.

"Look . . ." Lan wheezed, gazing over his shoulder. Ryan shifted around, relieved to see a large fishing trawler heading in their direction, its occupants calling out to them. The vessel was old and dilapidated, but had been painted bright blue and green. It had a festive appearance even though it looked ready to fall apart.

Lan was worried. "What do we do?"

"I don't think we have a choice. Let's just hope they're friendly."

When the trawler eventually pulled alongside them, the fishermen lowered nets from the side of the boat. Ryan helped Lan grab hold of one and, climbing it like a ladder, she made her way to the boat's deck where the fishermen pulled her aboard. Ryan followed, aware that out here in the middle of nowhere they'd have no easy way to escape if this went bad. At the top, rough hands grabbed him and hauled him over the rail.

Ryan and Lan lay on their backs, drenched and panting. Curious faces surrounded them on all sides, many of them decorated with white paint on their nose and cheeks. There were rough-skinned men and women here, and Ryan even saw several children. An extended family, all living together on this fishing boat. They seemed to view the rescue as something pretty remarkable.

Lan tried to speak to them, but she was having trouble communicating. After a moment, she explained: "They're Nachine—River Gypsies. They have their own language."

"How many languages does Andakar have?"

"Fifty or sixty. Maybe more. Their language and traditions are the only freedom some people have. They don't let go easily."

A gruff, weathered-looking man squatted in front of them, openly appraising these two strangers. He motioned for them to take off their shoes and socks to let them dry, then turned back to his family and crew, snapping orders. With backward glances and whispered exchanges, they did as told, preparing the nets and manning the boat.

"Do they all live onboard?" Ryan asked, checking out the boat. In addition to the fishing gear, the trawler had clotheslines with laundry hanging to dry, an outdoor cooking area, and a sitting area with small chairs. They'd even hung twinkly lights and colorful flags all around.

"They do for several months each year," Lan told him. "The rest of the time, they live in temporary villages along the riverbanks, usually with a bunch of other families. They work together to make it through the rainy months. It's not an easy life."

A woman approached with two wooden bowls filled with yellow rice and chunks of fresh, white fish. She smiled, urging them to eat. Ryan scooped a bite into his mouth and nodded his enthusiasm. The dish was delicious, garlic and spices giving it a tangy flavor.

"Are they always this nice to strangers?" he asked after swallowing.

"For Buddhists, being a good host is a form of reverence. We take it very seriously." For a few peaceful moments, they ate in silence, the heat from the morning sun quickly drying their soaked clothes.

Now that they had food, the captain, as Ryan now thought of him, wanted answers. He directed his questions to Lan, each of them struggling to make the other understand, and she managed to communicate that they were in trouble. The man's expression darkened. He could guess who was after them, and he kept looking at his family as if he was already worrying for their safety.

One of the fishermen called out, pointing across the horizon. The captain moved swiftly to the back of the vessel. Ryan and Lan set their bowls down, following.

In the distance, sweeping along the hills above the waterfall, a military helicopter headed in their direction. Ryan and Lan traded a worried glance. To Ryan, the captain's face was unreadable as he watched the helicopter making its way toward them, weaving erratically in its search.

Abruptly, the captain turned to his family and shouted more commands. They jumped into action, some casting nets while others threw out lines with yellow buoys attached. The woman who had brought the fish and rice gestured for them to follow her quickly.

She led them to the middle of the boat's deck where two young boys slid open a wooden portal, revealing a dark cavity. She indicated they should get inside, her gaze darting to the skyline as the *whomp-whomp-whomp* sound of the helicopter came closer. Ryan couldn't see inside, but they didn't have much choice. Going first, he dropped into the shadows, landing unevenly on several burlap bags.

A moment later, Lan landed beside him and then the door above slammed shut, leaving them in near-total darkness. It was a compartment used to store supplies—cramped, claustrophobic, and wickedly hot. Lan took Ryan's hand and held on tight. They stayed completely still as the powerful buzz of the helicopter got nearer, until it was right overhead.

For several nerve-racking seconds, the helicopter didn't move. The entire boat shook as it circled. Then, miraculously, the shaking subsided and the sound faded. The chopper was moving away.

Ryan let out a sigh of relief, not even realizing he'd been holding his breath.

CHAPTER 40

**LAZU RIVER,
ANDAKAR**

Ryan didn't know how he was going to get them out of Andakar now. The Thai border would be swarming with ASI soldiers, making it impossible to connect with the smuggler who was supposed to get them across.

One of the fishermen was rowing Ryan and Lan to shore in a small skiff that had been tied up at the back of the trawler. The helicopter had continued its search downriver, so they had taken the opportunity to make it to land. But once they got there, Ryan had no idea which way to head.

They needed a plan.

He removed the plastic Baggie with his passport and cell phone from around his stomach.

The Baggie was still sealed, everything inside just as dry as when he'd taped it on. Turning on the phone, Ryan hoped he could get a signal out here in the open. Thirty seconds later, with the skiff just reaching shore, Danny's number began to ring.

Ryan waited, but there was no answer. After four rings, it clicked over to voice mail. "Hey, it's me," Ryan said. "If you get this, I could use your help. Check your email, okay?" Thumbs flying over the keyboard, Ryan composed a message to Danny updating him on the situation. He needed a way out of Andakar, but he didn't even know exactly where he was. His phone had less than half the battery left, but Ryan told Danny he'd leave it on for a while. With any luck, Danny could use the cell tracker app and the phone's GPS to locate them and help find some way across the border.

Ryan hit send just as the boat touched the riverbank. Before they disembarked, the River Gypsy who had been rowing them handed them each a plastic bottle of water and a folded piece of cloth. Ryan unwrapped his package, finding several strips of dried meat and pieces of flatbread covered with sesame seeds. They thanked him for the food and jumped off, happy to be back on solid ground.

Lan looked up a small hill. "The captain said there are train tracks up top. They lead back toward the border."

"That has to be at least ten miles away."

"And they'll be looking for us everywhere."

Ryan wished he could think of some alternative. But the truth was, he didn't have any other ideas. Maybe his parents would have known what to do, but he had absolutely no clue.

Hearing the sound of the helicopter, Ryan turned and saw it heading back in their direction. The chopper had made its quick, initial sweep down the river but was now backtracking, moving slowly and searching more carefully. "We need to find cover," he said, guiding them toward the trees and brush that lined the shore.

The crack of gunfire exploded across the river. Ryan and Lan dove behind a tree. But the shots weren't aimed at them.

"No!" Lan called in alarm. The helicopter circled the fisherman in the skiff like a shark stalking its prey. The man was panicked, paddling furiously back toward the trawler.

Machine gunfire tore into the small boat and the fisherman was struck multiple times. Lan instinctively turned away from the slaughter, but

Ryan stared in horror.

The ASI had killed the man in cold blood.

And they weren't done yet. The chopper hovered, now focusing on the trawler and the rest of the River Gypsies. The tinny sound of a bullhorn carried across the water as the soldiers communicated with the fishing vessel.

Lan saw what was happening. "They're forcing them to land."

Downriver, Ryan spotted a clear area where it appeared the boat was being directed. As he watched, a small convoy of military jeeps raced along a winding road that led down to the landing point. The vehicles screeched to a stop and soldiers jumped out, weapons drawn as they waited for the trawler.

"The ASI," Ryan said.

"They'll torture them until someone breaks and admits they helped us. Then they'll kill them all."

Ryan looked up the hill. He knew the best chance for getting Lan and himself out of Andakar safely was to run the opposite direction and stay low. If they could get on a train, they'd be miles away in minutes.

Ryan thought of all the people he'd met over the last couple of days who had helped him: the monk with his string bracelet, the men at the café who didn't give him up, the prisoners at the ASI command center, the girl in the Hello Kitty shirt and her father. He would have never made it this far without each one. If he ran away now, it would feel like he was abandoning all of them.

Lan was right. Ryan couldn't live in a bubble. He couldn't just turn his back and pretend like this brutality wasn't happening. If he didn't help these people, who would?

"Get to the train tracks," Ryan told Lan. "Take whatever train comes along—just get out of here."

"We have to do something," she said.

"I'm gonna try, but you should go while you can. Otherwise, we'll probably both die here."

Lan held her ground. "I'm not going any-where."

Her mind was obviously made up. Ryan looked back at the trawler, which was being forced to shore by the gunmen aboard the helicopter. ASI soldiers waited for them, rifles pointed threateningly.

"You're sure?" Ryan asked.

"Positive."

"All right. I've actually got an idea. But I'll need your help."

CHAPTER
41

**NEW YORK,
USA**

Kasey didn't understand why the police sent only one squad car. When she made the anonymous call from the pay phone around the corner, she told the guy that she had heard a woman's scream coming from inside the building. She thought they'd send a SWAT team or something.

But it was just two uniformed officers who came to investigate. They knocked and rang a couple of buzzers. One of them stood on the sidewalk, peering up at the dark windows.

"What'll they do if no one answers?" Danny wondered.

"Maybe they'll call in reinforcements and search the building," Kasey said.

The front door unexpectedly opened and a light came on in the small foyer of the building. An Asian man in a cardigan sweater and reading glasses smiled at the officers. His back was slightly stooped and his movements were relaxed and deliberate. Kasey couldn't hear the conversation, but it all seemed very friendly.

"That's him," Danny said. "That's Aung Win."

Kasey was surprised. "That guy's a spy?" Aung Win invited the officers inside, then closed the front door.

"That's not what he looked like before. Believe me, he's totally evil."

"He just let the cops come in. Like he didn't have anything to worry about."

"Which means they're probably not gonna find anything. He's too smart. Maybe this was a mistake."

Kasey felt a sudden twinge of panic. Should they have waited to hear from Ryan? What if they had basically signed his mom's death warrant by calling the police? The next ten minutes felt like forever as they waited in silence. Occasionally, a light would come on in one of the empty apartments for a minute, then abruptly go back out.

Eventually, the front door opened again and

the officers and Aung Win emerged. Kasey's heart sank when she saw them all laughing. It hadn't worked.

The officers returned to their vehicle and drove away as Aung Win waved from the door. The moment the squad car disappeared, so did his smile. Aung Win stood up straight and pulled the glasses off.

"Get back!" Danny whispered, pulling Kasey deeper into the shadows.

They didn't move a muscle as Aung Win angrily glared up and down the block. After a few tense seconds, he stepped back inside and shut the door. The foyer light went out and the building was dark once more.

"What do we do now?" Kasey asked.

"We go home and pray we didn't screw everything up." Danny quickly began to disassemble the camera from his drone. "On a low setting, the camera records up to ten hours. We can hide it here aimed at the front door."

"You're gonna spy on the spy. Nice."

"I'll swing by before school in the morning and replace the memory card. At least we'll know if they leave."

They found a spot behind some pipes where the camera would be practically invisible and

Danny hit record.

They made sure nobody was watching from the building across the street. When they felt sure it was safe, they darted out of the alcove and turned to head down the sidewalk.

But their path was blocked by a tall, imposing figure.

"You're dead."

Danny gulped. It wasn't Aung Win, but it might be even worse: Kasey's brother Steeg glared at them, punching his fist into his free hand.

CHAPTER
42

**LAZU RIVER,
ANDAKAR**

An ASI officer, medals across his chest and gold epaulets adorning his shoulders, watched the trawler with a cold stare. As the boat approached shore, Ryan could make out the frightened faces of the River Gypsies, drifting ever closer to their doom.

This was his chance. All the soldiers were looking away from the jeeps and toward the water. Ryan nodded to Lan and they darted out of the trees, scurrying down the hill as quietly as possible. They crept in behind the last jeep.

"Is this enough?" she asked, showing him the handful of sticks and dried bamboo she had gathered.

"Perfect," Ryan said. "You ready? It's gonna happen fast."

"You really think this will work?" Lan looked dubiously at the plastic Baggie in Ryan's hand.

"I sure hope so." Ryan wasn't overly confident. They were going to need a big distraction to get the ASI's attention away from the fishing boat and this was the best idea he had.

Ryan had emptied the plastic Baggie holding his passport and phone, then filled it with the drinking water the fishermen had given them. He raised the Baggie of water up to the sun. As he hoped, the water inside the pouch created a makeshift lens, like a homemade magnifying glass. Holding it up to the sun's rays, Ryan created a laser-like beam of concentrated heat. It was an old survival trick he'd learned from his dad during a camping trip in Indonesia after their matches got wet in a storm.

Ryan focused the beam on the kindling. Seconds later, it burst into flames. "Okay," he whispered, "time for the bamboo. Be careful, it burns fast."

Lan put one end of the long, dry bamboo stick into the fire Ryan had created and it lit. Ryan peered around the jeep. The soldiers were still focused on the fishing boat.

He crept around the side of the jeep and un-screwed the gas cap. Lan slipped in beside him and placed the bamboo stick into the gas tank, leaving the burning end up top. The bamboo made a great natural fuse, the fire racing down its length.

But they had to get out of there *fast*! Ryan was running for the trees until Lan grabbed his hand and steered him behind a boulder. "Safer," she said.

With a *whoosh*, the gasoline in the tank ig-nited and the jeep burst into flames! Soldiers spun around in alarm, startled and confused by the sudden eruption.

Lan looked worried, though. "One jeep on fire won't stop them for long."

"The thing is, when you put fire in the gas tank, cars don't really explode like they do in the movies." Ryan grinned, making sure they were both fully behind the rock. "But the *hand grenades* in the back sure do. Cover your ears."

Lan did, as—*ka-boom!*—the first vehicle ex-ploded in a ball of fire! Soldiers scattered in all directions, jumping for cover. The officer was struck by the concussive blast, flying several feet in the air before he splashed down into the river. It was utter chaos, the fishing boat suddenly forgotten.

"Go!" Ryan yelled, pointing up the hillside. He and Lan took off running, getting as far away as possible while they could. As Lan continued, Ryan paused to look back.

After the initial pandemonium, the helicopter was wheeling around to come after them. But down below, a second jeep suddenly caught fire, triggered by the explosion of the first. As the chopper soared in their direction, the second jeep blew sky-high!

A chunk of flying metal hit the tail rotor and the helicopter began to veer wildly. It spun in circles, spiraling around and around until the tail hit a tree with a thunderous boom. The chopper plummeted to the ground like a brick, crashing right where Ryan and Lan had been hiding.

On the river, Ryan saw the fishing vessel swerve away from the shoreline and head back out to open water. Ryan hoped they'd get far, far away before any reinforcements could arrive.

Charging once more up the hill, Ryan caught up with Lan just as she made it to the top. Stopping to catch their breaths, they saw smoke billowing everywhere. It looked like a war zone.

Lan shook her head. "You sure you've never done this before?"

"Beginner's luck," Ryan said, with a smile. The sound of a train whistle stole their attention from the destruction by the river. They had made it to the tracks the captain told them about, and a train was chugging right toward them. Ryan was excited, thinking they'd finally caught a break.

But Lan immediately dashed his hopes. "It's heading the wrong direction—*away* from the border. Toward China."

Ryan thought through their options. The explosions would only distract the ASI long enough for them to radio for help. And he knew the Thai borders were basically impossible to cross. So maybe it was time do something unexpected. Maybe it was time to leave his father's plan behind and trust in himself.

With the train coming closer, they had to act quickly. "We should take it. It's our best chance to shake the ASI."

Lan didn't hesitate. "I'm with you."

Together, they sprinted toward the passing train.

CHAPTER
43

**THANLIN,
ANDAKAR**

Tasha hoped she wasn't too late.

It had taken most of the night to shake the ASI soldiers chasing her. Twice, she'd been cornered and feared it was the end. But Tasha Levi never gave up. She knew how to fight with a viciousness that stunned the soldiers. Underestimating her was a serious mistake. She'd left a few dead bodies behind her, but had no regrets.

Whatever it took to accomplish her mission.

When she was finally safe, Tasha had doubled back around to Thanlin. She found the villager she had seen with Ryan and forced him to tell her about the temple with the secret chamber. Moving fast, she had traversed the mountain in a couple of hours, hoping to find Ryan and John Quinn still in hiding.

The temple grounds appeared to be empty. Tasha identified the golden dome the villager had mentioned and headed that way. But the rumble of a motor stopped her in her tracks.

A jeep was approaching from the opposite end. Tasha pressed up against a temple wall and tracked its progress. It pulled to a stop and two soldiers got out. The men wore gray uniforms, which meant they weren't ASI. Probably just a regular guard patrol. They appeared relaxed as they set off in opposite directions.

Tasha needed that jeep. If John and Ryan Quinn weren't already gone, it would make the next leg of the journey much simpler. She couldn't afford for the guards to raise the alarm and bring more soldiers. Which meant they'd have to be eliminated.

Silent as a cat, Tasha followed the driver as he wound his way through the temple structures. After a few minutes, he stopped and unstrapped his rifle, leaning it against a wall. He took a couple of steps around the corner, unzipping his pants. This was going to be too easy.

Thinking he was alone, the soldier peed, whistling softly. Tasha crept forward, closing the distance between them. She picked up his rifle, holding it like a club. He was zipping his pants back up as she advanced, swinging the weapon like a baseball bat. *Whack!* The butt of the rifle hit the driver on the back of the head and he crumpled to the ground. When he tried to get up, Tasha struck him again.

She dropped the rifle and took the soldier's handgun instead, tucking it into her pants against the small of her back. Searching his pockets, she found the jeep keys, then hurried to locate the second soldier.

Hearing his heavy steps, Tasha slipped into the shadows of a temple entrance. After the soldier passed, she snuck behind him and wrapped her forearm around his neck in a choke hold. The startled guard struggled, but her grip only tightened. He dropped to his knees, fingers clawing at her arm. A few seconds later, his eyes rolled up into his head and he went limp.

That's what happens when you're careless and undisciplined, she thought.

Tasha drove the jeep to the entrance of the gold-domed temple and jumped back out. Inside, she found the wall sculpture the villager had described and pushed. Slowly, it opened, pivoting to reveal the tunnel's entrance. Absolute silence greeted Tasha.

She was too late—they'd already gone.

But as she stepped into the chamber, her senses went on high alert. She whirled around, drawing the handgun from her pants with one smooth motion.

"Don't shoot. It's just me." John Quinn leaned against the wall.

"Quinn!" she said, not disguising the relief she felt at seeing him alive. Then she glanced around and realized, "You're alone?"

"Ryan found me. I was surprised when he said you'd helped him get here. How did you know where I was?"

"I didn't. I went to find you and sort of walked into a mess. Where's Ryan?"

"With any luck, he and the girl I was helping are in Thailand by now. I need to call Simon McClelland and make sure they made contact."

"We'll call as soon as we can get a signal." Tasha noticed the bandages. "You're injured."

"I'm getting stronger," John insisted. "With your help, I can travel."

"Good," Tasha said, coming around behind him. "Because we have somewhere to be."

Tasha pulled what appeared to be a pen out of her pocket. She'd been carrying it since they landed in Andakar. But it wasn't a pen at all. It was a well-disguised hypodermic needle filled with enough tranquilizer to subdue a sumo wrestler. It would be plenty for John Quinn.

She plunged the needle into John's neck. He turned to her in shock and confusion as the drug flooded his body.

"What?" he stammered, already unsteady. "Why . . . ?"

"You'll find out soon enough," Tasha said without a trace of compassion. John crumpled to the ground, unconscious. Tasha smiled.

Mission accomplished.

CHAPTER
44

**CHINDI PROVINCE,
ANDAKAR**

*T*he train rattled along, rocking back and forth so gently that it had lulled Lan to sleep. For the first time since they'd met, Ryan thought she seemed at peace. He looked back out the window. Along the way, the scenery had shifted from verdant mountain jungle to flat plains and was now changing once more. If things were different, Ryan imagined the rolling hills and forests they were passing through would be fun to explore.

The train was huge, probably close to a hundred cars long, and filled mostly with locals who appeared to be from rural areas. Jumping onboard hadn't been hard. The train was slow enough that Ryan and Lan were able to run alongside and grab the handrails on the back car. Luckily, nobody was checking tickets, so they were able to find empty seats and blend into the crowd.

Ryan's phone vibrated in his pocket. He slipped it out, thankful to see he finally had a signal again. It was Danny. It was almost noon here in Andakar, which meant it was close to midnight back in New York. Not wanting to wake Lan, Ryan moved down the aisle before answering.

"Hey."

"Dude, you're going the wrong way!" Danny said, skipping hellos. "I've got your GPS up on my tracking program—you need to turn around, like *now*."

Just hearing his friend's voice made Ryan feel a little better. "We ran into a few problems."

"The kind where you're dodging bullets?"

"Plus some white-water rapids, military choppers, and exploding hand grenades. And that's just since this morning."

"You're joking."

"So not joking."

"Wow," Danny said. "And here I was feeling all impressed with myself that I fought with Steeg tonight."

"You fought Steeg?" Ryan knew that couldn't have gone well. "Are you okay?"

"Well, by *fought*, what I really mean is, 'ran as fast as possible in the opposite direction.' So, yeah, I'm fine."

"You need to stay away from that guy." Ryan glanced over at Lan, still sleeping. "Did you get my email?"

"Yeah—so Myat Kaw is a girl, huh?" Danny said, and Ryan knew what was coming next: "Is she hot?"

"You're unbelievable."

"She is, isn't she? Text me a pic!"

"How about I just let you see her for yourself? All you have to do is find us a way out of here."

Ryan could hear Danny clicking away on his keyboard as he spoke. "Are you on a train?" he asked.

"Yeah, how'd you know that?"

"I've got your GPS location on satellite now. I can see the tracks."

"Lan says we're headed for China." Ryan glanced over and noticed one of the passengers, an older man with a brutish face, watching him. Ryan nodded a friendly hello, then turned away, hoping the man would lose interest.

"She's right. You're actually within a few miles of the Chinese border now."

"How close is the nearest airport?"

Danny typed again. "In Jinhong, about fifty miles from the border. They have an international airport that gets lots of tourists. You wouldn't stand out."

"Then that's where we need to go. If I send you the names on our passports, you think you could figure out a way to get us a couple of tickets?"

"I'll make it happen. And I'll send you a satellite map of the border area. It looks like a lot of forest and hills around there."

"I'm not sure how long my battery will last. I'll have to turn off the phone until we're close, make sure I have enough juice left to get whatever info you send about flights."

"Listen," Danny said. "Things have been pretty crazy here, too. I may know where your mom is being held."

Ryan totally forgot to keep his voice down. "You saw her?"

"No, but I saw Aung Win and that big dude with him." Danny told him about the apartment building. They didn't know for sure if Jacqueline was inside, but it seemed likely. The fact that

Kasey was now involved came as a shock. But just then another call started beeping through.

He glanced at the screen and his stomach churned: "Blocked."

"I gotta go—I think it's him calling," Ryan told Danny.

"Ryan, wait!" Danny's tone was so urgent that Ryan hesitated. "We called the cops. We were just trying to help—but it didn't work."

"Oh no . . ." Was Aung Win calling to tell him that he'd already done what he promised? Was his mother dead?

"I'm sorry, we really thought—"

"I have to go." Ryan hit the accept button on his phone, fearing what was to come. "Hello?"

"My instructions were very clear." Aung Win's voice was unmistakable. "You were not to speak to anyone."

"I only talked to my dad, just like you told me." Ryan hoped it was convincing since it was the truth.

"You called the police!"

"I didn't. I promise."

Aung Win remained suspicious. "It would be foolish of you not to do as I say."

"I know that. My dad told me to just do exactly what you tell me to. Is my mom okay?"

"What does it matter? You are out of time."

"We have one more day! You said five days—that's tomorrow." Ryan knew one day wouldn't be enough time for Dad to get back, but he'd worry about that later. Right now, he had to make Aung Win believe everything was fine. "My father said to tell you he has Myat Kaw. He has your niece."

Aung Win said nothing. Ryan let it sink in that he knew Myat Kaw's identity, then continued, "He said he'll make the trade. Your niece for my mom. As long as my mother isn't hurt. I'm supposed to talk to her, to make sure she's okay."

"He wants to know if you're okay," Aung Win said, but he wasn't speaking to Ryan.

And then he heard his mom's voice: "Don't trust him, Ryan! Tell Dad not to—" But her final words were muffled, like a gag had been placed over her mouth. Ryan was surprised at how calm he remained, not rattled like the last call.

"If anything happens to her, the deal is off," Ryan said.

"And if anyone learns Myat Kaw's true identity before she is in my possession, then she is useless to me. And so is your mother." Aung Win's tone became brisk and efficient. "Tell

John Quinn I will contact him at this number to-morrow. He will have one opportunity to make the trade according to my instructions. Alone. Any deviation and I will simply disappear. Along with your mother."

"Ryan!" Ryan turned to find Lan just behind him. She was worried, glancing back the way she'd come. At the end of the train car, the older passenger who had stared at Ryan was pointing him out to a uniformed police officer.

"Do you understand?" Aung Win snapped in Ryan's ear. Ryan felt like a traitor, arranging to trade Lan to a man who wanted to kill her while she looked at him as an ally.

"I got it," he said to Aung Win. The connection was immediately terminated. Lan gave him a curious look. "That was Danny," he lied. "He's gonna help us get out of here."

The officer was now talking into a radio—they had to move.

"This way," Ryan said, moving to the back of the car. He opened the exit door and stepped out between the train cars. Beneath his feet, the ground rushed past as wind whipped his face. He grabbed hold of the handle on the opposite side and stepped across the open space to the next car.

They charged down the aisle, passing from car to car. But the police officer was gaining on them. Pushing Lan ahead of him, Ryan grabbed a couple of suitcases and baskets of vegetables that lined the sides, knocking them into the officer's path to slow his pursuit.

Passengers jumped up and yelled after Ryan angrily, causing even more difficulty for the officer. Ryan made it to the back of the car, just as Lan opened the next door. But she froze in the doorway: They were at the end of the line, nothing beyond but empty air.

They didn't even hesitate. Ryan and Lan jumped!

CHAPTER

45

**CHINDI PROVINCE,
ANDAKAR**

Ryan knew to hit the ground in a roll to lessen the impact. But when he got up, he saw that Lan had landed harder. He helped her up, and she winced.

"Your ankle?" he asked.

"It's all right." She put weight on it, but it obviously hurt.

Screeeeech! The squeal of the train's metal brakes was ear-piercing as it slowed to a stop. Ryan pointed toward the forest up the hill.

"There. We can hide." He offered Lan a hand, but she refused. Moving as fast as they were able, they hurried toward the cover of the trees. Behind them, passengers stuck their heads out the windows and watched the unexpected excitement.

The forest was dense, and the train was soon out of sight. They stopped so Lan could rest her ankle a few minutes and Ryan could check the map Danny sent. The Chinese border was only a few miles away, but it was hilly terrain. Unfortunately, Ryan's phone now showed a single bar left on the battery. Not only would they lose their map, they'd also lose all contact with Danny if it ran out of power. Ryan took another minute to try and memorize the map, then reluctantly turned the phone off.

For the next hour, they trekked through the forest, moving steadily uphill. Hungry and exhausted, it took all their strength, both physically and mentally, to just keep moving forward. When a helicopter buzzed by overhead, they knew the ASI had been alerted and was now searching the area.

Making it to the top of a ridge, Ryan scanned the valley below. It was a rustic area, full of trees and jagged boulders. Cows, oxen, and horses grazed in grassy clearings. At the bottom of the basin was a small community of wood-thatched homes and simple barns. Rocky hills encroached on both sides, and there was just one road in and out—a road that looked like their only possibility of escape. It led to the border crossing at the far end of town, where heavily armed soldiers stopped anyone trying to leave Andakar.

"We can't get across here," Lan said, disheartened. "There are too many of them."

Ryan felt his own doubt grow as a chopper flew past. Down below, more soldiers arrived, jumping out of their jeeps. They searched the houses and barns, treating the citizens roughly. Ryan and Lan were severely outmatched. It would be suicide to attempt a border crossing here, but there was nowhere else to go.

Ryan thought of Varian Fry and the original Emergency Rescue Committee, who helped save so many people from the Nazis, knowing they'd be killed if they were caught. They must have been scared, too. There must have been times when escape seemed impossible. His own grandfather probably felt like this—and his parents, too.

He glanced over at Lan, whose eyes were closed, her head slightly bowed as she muttered under her breath. After a moment, she looked up and saw Ryan watching her.

"Were you praying?" he asked.

"Buddhists don't pray. I was giving thanks for a blessing."

Ryan was confused. "Is there a blessing in this that I'm missing?"

"You're the blessing," she said. "You and your father. Whatever happens next, the two of you allowed me to hope again—if only for a little while."

Ryan fixed her with steely gaze. "That sounds a lot like you're giving up."

Her only answer was to look up at the helicopter, which was sweeping toward them. As it spun around, the chopper's side door slid open and a soldier appeared, shouting through a bullhorn. Another soldier appeared beside him and aimed a rifle their direction.

"They want us to come out," Lan said.

No way, Ryan thought. He wasn't giving up—and he wasn't letting Lan give up, either. He'd spotted something down the hill that had sparked an idea, a way they might still be able to get out of this. Ryan grabbed Lan's hand, pulling her after him.

"Run!" he yelled. "Stay close to the trees!" A shot rang out, splintering a branch behind them, as Ryan pulled her into a thicket. They heard another couple of shots, but they weren't as close.

He kept changing directions, always keeping the trees between them and the helicopter.

"Where are we going?" Lan asked breathlessly, fighting the pain in her injured ankle. "There's no way we can get through the border crossing."

"We're not going to," Ryan answered. "We're going around it!" Ryan veered sharply to their right, taking them in a completely different direction than they'd been heading. Since the chopper couldn't see them through the trees, he hoped this would confuse their hunt.

It worked. The helicopter moved away, not realizing its targets were now on a different path. But Ryan could hear the rumble of truck engines racing up the narrow roads. The ASI soldiers were on the way.

Ryan stopped abruptly as they neared the edge of the trees. He had skirted around the hill with this destination in mind. Fifty yards away was one of the ranches he'd spotted. That's where he hoped to find their possible ticket to freedom.

"There." Ryan pointed, enjoying the light that came to Lan's eyes when she realized what he was thinking:

"Horses!" Lan looked genuinely excited. "I'm

an excellent rider," she said. "You, too?"

"No," Ryan admitted, "I'm terrible. But if you can swim the rapids and run on a hurt ankle, I can stay on a horse."

Three horses were tethered on the far side of the clearing. Crouching low, Ryan and Lan used the huge humpbacked cows as cover, weaving among them as they approached the horses.

As they arrived, Ryan realized the horses had reins, but no saddles. Riders here only used simple blankets thrown over the horse's back. Lan seemed used to that, leaping onto the back of a beautiful chestnut-colored mare in one agile motion. Ryan wasn't as graceful, hoisting himself onto a gray stallion and nearly sliding off the other side. He finally got settled and pulled on the reins, prodding the horse with his heels to get it running. The horse bolted forward, nearly throwing Ryan off as it chased after Lan.

"Across the field and up the hill," Ryan called. "We make it to the other side and we'll be in China!"

Lan was a confident rider, and she charged across the open clearing. Ryan barely stayed seated as his gray stallion flew after her. But after a few seconds of breakneck galloping, he fell into the horse's rhythm and the ride felt more natural. He glanced back, seeing the helicopter execute a wide arc in pursuit of them.

"They're coming!" he yelled. "Get to the trees!"

Lan knew what she was doing, using the reins to guide her horse in that direction. Thankfully, Ryan's stallion seemed happy to follow, allowing him to focus on hanging on. They had almost made it across the field when the chopper swooped in, soldiers firing from the open doorway. Bullets hit the ground on all sides, a few of them barely missing before the horses reached the tree line and disappeared into the forest. The chopper flew overhead so low that Ryan felt his whole body shake.

Gripping the horse with his legs and the reins with his fists, Ryan struggled to keep upright. These were mountain horses, used to the rocky hillside they were now climbing. They darted between the trees, nimbly keeping their footing over the rough terrain. Limbs and twigs struck Ryan's body and face as Lan led them ever higher, taking them around the border crossing down below.

Finally, they crested the top, pausing for a moment to look back. From up here, they could see the frustrated ASI soldiers in their jeeps, unable to follow because no roads led this high. The chopper continued crisscrossing the sky, trying to find them.

"Do you see where we are?" Ryan asked.

Lan looked at the border crossing down in the valley and then realized: "China! We're over the border—we made it!"

Ryan grinned, then glanced warily at the helicopter. "We'd better keep moving. They probably won't risk flying into Chinese airspace, but I wouldn't want to bet on it."

Reining the horses around, they started down the other side, using the forest for cover. As they rode on for the next hour, the reality finally settled in: They had actually done it—they were out of Andakar.

But Ryan's relief was short-lived as he remembered the impossible choice that would soon face him. He had promised to trade Lan for his mother. Aung Win had given him only until tomorrow, which meant that his dad wouldn't make it back in time to help. Which was a disaster because Ryan had no idea how to handle this.

When he left New York, he believed he would do whatever it took to save his mom. His family meant everything to him. There was no sacrifice he wouldn't make.

But then he'd met Lan. Small and delicate on the outside, but with a rebel's heart. She was just a teenager, but she'd already been through so much and faced it with strength and courage.

Aung Win demanded a trade. It had to be one or the other.

Would he save Lan or his mother?

How was he supposed to choose?

PART FOUR

DO OR DIE

CHAPTER 46

**NEW YORK,
USA**

Home.

For Ryan, it was weird to think of any one place that way. But as the taxi sped from the airport toward Manhattan and he caught his first glimpse of the skyline, that's exactly how he felt. For the last couple of years, Ryan had been craving a home and now he had one.

But what good was a home without the family to fill it?

Lan rode next to him, her face pressed against the glass, taking in the strange, new surroundings with a mixture of awe and panic. It was Saturday morning in New York, a crisp autumn day without a cloud in the sky. Traffic was light as they zipped along the expressway. On the long flight back, they had both eaten and slept, though Ryan's slumber had been filled with fitful dreams.

Thanks to Danny's hard work, catching the plane out of China had been the smoothest part of this entire experience. He had booked tickets under the fake identities on the passports Ryan and Lan carried. At the airport, they had blended into the crowds of tourists without any issues. Danny had also wired money to the Western Union station at the airport, enough for them to buy food and new clothes at the gift shops. A sandwich and a fresh change of underwear and socks had been desperately needed!

Ryan checked his phone once more, making sure he hadn't received a message from his dad. No text, no email, no voice mail. No contact at all. Ryan hoped he was all right, but mostly, he wished he'd get in touch to tell Ryan what to do. Aung Win could call at any moment to arrange the trade of Myat Kaw for Jacqueline. When he did, Ryan would have to act quickly.

Lan turned from the taxi's window. "On the train, that was my uncle you were talking to, wasn't it?"

The question caught Ryan off guard, but he

didn't even consider lying to her. They'd been through too much together. "Yeah."

"And he'll trade your mother for me?"

Ryan nodded. "That's what he says, anyway. My mom yelled out not to trust him."

"She's right." Lan had a determined look on her face. "But you have to make the trade anyway. We have to do whatever we can to save your mom."

Ryan could tell she meant it. Despite the risk, Lan was ready to go with her uncle, to do anything necessary to help—to give up her own life to save someone else.

And in that moment, Ryan knew there was no way he could ever let Aung Win get his hands on Lan.

Ryan flashed back on all that had happened: He'd used a fake ID to sneak into a hostile country, broken into the command center of a spy agency, and journeyed across rivers and mountains while being chased by jerks with machine guns. Five days ago, he would've never believed any of that was possible. But he'd done it. And somehow, he'd figure this out, too.

There had to be a way to save them both.

Daylight vanished as they plunged into the Midtown Tunnel, which led under the East River and into Manhattan. White tiles flashed past in the dimly lit underpass. Ryan wished he had a deck of cards. Practicing his sleight-of-hand tricks always helped him think.

Ryan opened up the email program on his phone, which was now fully recharged. Danny had sent him photos of the building where they believed his mom was being held. Danny's camera had been recording the entrance ever since the failed police search. Neither Aung Win nor the bodyguard had come out, but the driver of their car had stopped by twice. He brought several bags of groceries on each visit, which made Ryan believe they were still holed up inside. Probably lying low until the trade.

Suddenly, Ryan stopped.

The trade . . . the driver . . . sleight-of-hand . . .

His thoughts came in a jumble as a plan began to form. He couldn't do it on his own. He'd need the help of his friends to pull it off, but Ryan finally felt a glimmer of hope.

As the taxi pulled out of the tunnel and into traffic, Ryan started putting the pieces together.

CHAPTER

47

**NEW YORK,
USA**

ack home, Ryan ran straight for his parents' room and unearthed the canister of pepper spray from his mom's gym bag. She kept it with her workout clothes and running shoes—just in case.

Stuffing the canister in his pocket, he hurried down the hallway of his family's brownstone to his bedroom. He went straight to the pegboard that held all his baseball caps. Without hesitation, he grabbed his Roy Halladay–signed Philadelphia Phillies hat and pulled it on. Halladay had thrown a no-hitter his very first time pitching during the playoffs—the first post-season no-hitter in over fifty years. It was the kind of once-in-a-lifetime success that Ryan needed today. He hoped the cap brought him the same luck.

As he came back downstairs, the doorbell rang. He glanced through the peephole, then opened the door, happy to see Danny on the front steps.

"Thanks for coming," Ryan said. Just seeing his friend standing there gave him a boost of confidence, which he sorely needed.

"Yeah, it was either join my parents for a day of antiques shopping, or come here and help you kick some butt. You're lucky antiques suck."

"Antiques may sound better before today's over."

Danny's cool bravado disappeared as he grabbed Ryan in a spontaneous hug. "Dude, it's good to see you. I thought for sure you were a goner."

Ryan grinned. "Thanks for keeping that to yourself."

"Ryan!" The guys pulled apart, turning to see Kasey arrive. "I'm so glad you're okay."

"Sorry you got pulled into all this," Ryan said.

"I'm not. And whatever you need, we're here for you." She turned as Steeg came up behind her, scowling.

Danny instinctively stepped behind Ryan,

using him as a human shield. "Back off, man, or Ryan'll go all ninja on you!"

"Ignore him," Ryan said, stepping forward and stretching out his hand to Steeg. "We never officially met. I'm Ryan—thanks for helping."

"I haven't agreed to anything yet." But Steeg reluctantly shook Ryan's hand.

Danny looked between them, confused. "What's going on?"

"That's what I want to know." Steeg glanced at his sister, then back to Ryan. "All this stuff she told me—it's some kinda prank, right?"

"I wish. I know it sounds crazy, but it's real."

"We brought my parents' car like you asked," Kasey said.

"We're not going anywhere with these guys." Steeg was adamant, used to being in charge. "No way I'm risking my license on some stupid scheme that's probably a bunch of bull anyway."

"Before anyone decides to do anything or not, I want you to meet someone." He ushered them inside the brownstone, quickly scanning the street for anyone suspicious before he closed the door.

Ryan led everyone down the hall to the kitchen where Lan was typing on Ryan's laptop. He said Lan's name to get her attention, and she looked up with a fierce expression. All it took for her to change from a frightened teenager to the crusading blogger Myat Kaw was a laptop and internet access.

"I started several rumors that Myat Kaw had been taken prisoner by an American," she said. "That should make my uncle more confident the trade is happening."

"Good. Everyone, this is Lan." Ryan introduced Danny and Kasey, adding, "These are the two who managed to get us out of the country."

"Thanks," Lan said. "Ryan's lucky to have such smart friends."

Danny grinned. "And handsome—don't forget how handsome his friends are. And very available to show you around this amazing city."

"Seriously?" Steeg just shook his head.

"Well, I don't mean, like, *right now*."

"Danny showed me the blogs you've been writing," Kasey said. "It's amazing. You're really helping people."

"I just write the truth."

"Well, the truth can be powerful in the right hands." Kasey didn't hide her admiration.

Ryan noticed that Steeg was uncharacteristically quiet, his eyes never leaving Lan. "This is Kasey's brother, Steeg."

"Nice to meet you." Steeg held out his hand, which Lan took delicately, not used to the gesture. "And it's, uh, Drew. My name—it's Drew."

"Hello, Drew." Lan actually blushed as Steeg broke into a goofy smile, the two holding hands longer than necessary. "It's nice to meet you, too."

"You gotta be kidding." Danny rolled his eyes. Maybe convincing Steeg to help wouldn't be that hard, after all.

Ryan brought everyone up to speed on all that had happened, answering their many questions. Ryan was impatient, knowing they might not have much time. But if everyone wasn't on the same page, they didn't stand a chance of succeeding.

Finally, Ryan was ready to tell them what he had in mind.

"When I was a kid," he started, "my dad encouraged me to learn magic. Sleight of hand, card tricks, making things look like they can float. You know what the most critical part of any magic trick is?"

"Finding someone to watch who's not bored to tears?" Danny suggested.

"Distraction," Ryan said. "You have to get your audience focused in one direction"—Ryan snapped with the fingers of his left hand and they all glanced that way—"while the *real* trick is happening someplace completely different."

Ryan's strategy required an element of surprise, so they'd only have one shot to get it right. A million things could go wrong. But he forced himself not to think about those now. This plan had to work.

His mother's life depended on it.

CHAPTER
48

**NEW YORK,
USA**

yan's cell phone rang as the screen lit up with the word he'd been anxiously awaiting: "Blocked."

The call had finally come. Still no contact from Dad or Tasha. Ryan was beginning to give up hope that she'd escaped or that his father would make it out of Andakar. But he couldn't allow those worries to control him. He had to keep moving forward. Ryan picked up the phone and held it out to Steeg.

"You ready?"

Steeg took it, nervous. "This whole acting thing, I don't know . . ."

Kasey gave his arm a reassuring squeeze. "You can do it, Drew. Just be tough and determined—pretend it's the final seconds of a playoff game."

Steeg nodded, psyching himself up. The three of them were on the second floor of a massive used bookstore, tucked in a private corner next to a picture window. The bookstore was across the street from the building where they'd seen Aung Win and the bodyguard. Danny had checked the camera one last time and believed they were all still inside.

As the phone rang again, Steeg answered, putting the call on speaker so Ryan and Kasey could hear. He took a deep breath and said, "This is John Quinn."

Ryan prayed this would work. Being seventeen and a big guy, Steeg's voice had already changed, giving him the lower register of a grown man. They needed Aung Win to believe he was dealing directly with Ryan's father.

"You have Myat Kaw?" Aung Win's gravelly voice was unmistakable.

"I want to speak to my wife." Steeg did well, his tone confident and assured. "I won't hand over your niece unless I know she's okay."

For an interminable few seconds there was no response, and Ryan felt a twinge of panic. He heard a scuffling sound as the phone was moved, and then his mom's voice, tense but controlled: "John, is that you?"

Ryan pointed to the name *Jackie* written on a notepad for Steeg. Ryan's father always called her Jacqueline, never a nickname. He hoped this would send a signal to his mom to play along.

"It's me, *Jackie*," Steeg said. "Are you okay?"

Jacqueline only hesitated a moment, then said, "I'm fine, Johnny." Ryan gave a silent cheer—his mom had understood, sending back her own signal by calling his dad Johnny. Hopefully, that meant she'd be on the alert, ready for them when they moved into action.

Aung Win was back. "You will deliver Lan to me. You have her?"

"I do," Steeg answered. Kasey gave him a thumbs-up. She made a mean face, encouraging her brother to stay tough and in character. "My wife better not be hurt."

"As long as you don't contact the authorities, she will be unharmed. Come alone." His tone was cold and detached. Ryan wished he could reach through the phone and punch him.

"Where?" Steeg asked.

"There is a private airfield on Long Island. The East Shore Aerodrome. Bring her there."

"You have to promise me you won't kill Lan.

She's just a girl." That was a nice touch, Ryan thought. Steeg was really selling it.

"You have two hours," Aung Win said, and the call was disconnected.

Steeg gave the phone to Ryan, then looked at his hand. "I'm shaking. I never shake."

"You were perfect," Ryan assured him. "He totally bought it."

Kasey was already standing. "We need to get in position. I'll find Danny and Lan." She took off to collect the other two, who had been killing time while they waited for the call, lost in the vast collection of used books.

Ryan got up, but Steeg stopped him. "Listen, I get that it's a lot to deal with, what your parents are going through and all. But are you sure this is the right play? Maybe we should just leave it to the cops."

"Aung Win will be on the lookout for police. I can't risk him getting spooked. But he won't be expecting any problems from a bunch of kids."

"That's because a bunch of kids shouldn't be doing this."

Ryan understood Steeg's reluctance. He still felt it himself. "You want me to tell Kasey to go home?"

"Nobody tells Kasey to do anything she

doesn't want to do. But since my job is to be with Danny and Lan, it's up to you to watch out for her, got it? Forget about this Aung Win dirtbag—anything happens to Kasey and you've got *me* to worry about." After a beat to let that sink in, he walked away.

Steeg was right. Ryan was putting his friends in danger. Sure, he thought he had figured out a way to keep everyone safe, but what if things didn't go as planned? What if everything fell apart and someone got hurt?

"You coming?" Kasey was once again at Ryan's side. Beyond her, he saw Danny, Steeg, and Lan waiting at the top of the stairs.

"I can't ask you guys to do this."

"We're all here because we chose to be," Kasey said.

"But it's not your problem."

"Of course it is. You're our friend, and you need help. That's what friends do."

"It's too dangerous."

"How dangerous was getting Lan out of Andakar? And what about your parents? Who knows how much they've risked helping people over the years."

"That's different," Ryan said. "They knew

what they were getting into."

"So do we," Kasey insisted. "Isn't that the point of the Emergency Rescue Committee? That sometimes it's worth taking risks to help people when they really need it?"

"Your brother thinks we should just leave it to the cops."

"That's what I thought, too," Kasey said. "I was the one who pushed Danny to call them that night, and it was almost a disaster. These guys are smart and careful. I think your plan is the best chance we've got to get your mom away from them safely."

"You do?" Ryan was surprised by how much her vote of confidence meant to him.

"Absolutely."

Ryan felt a renewed sense of commitment. "All right—let's do this. But just in case, have 911 ready to dial, okay?"

"Will do. But this is gonna work."

"I hope you're right."

"I better be," Kasey said, "because we have a date for the Autumn Carnival Dance tonight."

"That's tonight?" Ryan had completely for-gotten.

Kasey arched an eyebrow playfully: "Don't

think for a second that all this gets you out of dancing with me."

Together, they joined the others and headed downstairs.

There was no turning back now.

CHAPTER 49

NEW YORK, USA

Timing would be everything. Their crucial advantage was that Aung Win would not anticipate any problems here at his safe house. If something were to go wrong, he'd expect it to happen at the airfield during the trade.

At least, that's what Ryan hoped.

Ryan and Kasey were at the corner, a short distance from the building's front door. Ryan had checked the video Danny recorded and confirmed that there was no back entrance. They would have to bring his mother out the front.

"When it goes down, everything's gonna happen fast," Ryan told Kasey. "Stay here and wait for my mom. I'll try to buy you as much time as I can to get her to the car."

"Got it," Kasey said, opening her bag. "I grabbed everything I could think of that might help cut her free. Scissors if her hands are duct-taped, wire cutters if they have her zip-tied. And if she's in handcuffs"—she produced a bobby pin bent into an L-shape—"one ready-to-go lockpick."

Kasey was full of surprises. "You know how to pick a lock?"

"I have three brothers who love to play tricks on me. I learned a while ago how to break into their rooms and get my revenge."

"Remind me not to mess with you," Ryan said. "Okay, you're the lookout. I'm gonna get set."

Ryan pulled his Phillies cap out of his back pocket and put it on, tugging the brim down low. He grabbed the sleeping bag and card-board box he'd brought from home. The box was a big one from their recent move. Ryan had pierced several holes in it for spying. In a nook a few doors down from Aung Win's build-ing, he set it up to look like a homeless person's shelter. He left the end of his sleeping bag vis-ible and threw some fast-food wrappers down to make it convincing.

Danny had downloaded an app on all their phones that allowed them to be used as walkie-talkies. Ryan put one headphone in his ear and, with the press of a button, had instant communication with the group.

"Everybody in place?"

"It's cold up here." Shrill and loud, Danny's voice bellowed through the headphone, causing Ryan to quickly lower the volume. "Can you see me?"

Ryan peeked out of his cardboard hideout, looking toward the roof. Leaning against the edge, five stories up, he saw Danny waving. The brick building was narrow, only four windows across, with a fire escape that had a landing at each level. After the top platform, a metal ladder led to the roof.

"I see you," Ryan confirmed. "How's Lan?"

"Great. We're getting to spend some quality time together." Danny's voice lowered to a whisper. "I think she's really into me."

Steeg's voice broke through. "You know we can all hear you, right?"

"Jealous, big guy?" Danny mocked, enjoying himself.

"Hey, everybody," Kasey interrupted. "Heads

up. Somebody's coming out."

Ryan ducked back inside his cardboard box. Through a hole, he watched as the door opened. A moment later, Aung Win appeared. He had on the cardigan and glasses Danny had described. Stooped over, he carried a broom in his hand. He began sweeping, but Ryan could tell he was actually scanning the area for signs of trouble.

His gaze swept toward Ryan's makeshift homeless shelter. Ryan pulled away from the eyehole, staying completely still. He held the canister of pepper spray, ready to fire.

But nothing happened.

"He's going back in." Kasey's voice was quiet. Several minutes passed. It seemed like forever to Ryan.

And finally: "Diplomatic plates coming this way."

Through an eyehole, he watched the familiar black Town Car pull to a stop in front of the building. The driver stepped out and scanned the street. He waited until a couple of pedestrians had walked past, then moved around to the rear door.

Ryan pressed the button on his cell-walkie, his voice barely a whisper. "It's showtime."

CHAPTER 50

**NEW YORK,
USA**

L an had a secret.

She wasn't sure why she hadn't told Ryan. There'd been plenty of time as they traveled. Maybe it was because it still hurt too much.

But now, she was going to use that secret to hopefully do some good.

Up on the roof, Danny turned to her. "You ready?"

She nodded, sticking one headphone into her ear, then slipped the phone he'd lent her into a pocket. She climbed onto the ladder and started down. It was old and rickety, shaking a little as she descended to the top level of the fire escape.

She heard Danny's voice in her ear. "Lan's on the move."

Though everyone had a part to play, Lan's role was critical. She was to provide the distraction Ryan needed. If she accomplished her goal, it would give Ryan enough time to grab his mother and get her away from Aung Win and his men.

Now, it was Ryan's voice in her ear. "Don't go any lower than the third story," he said. "I don't want you getting too close to him."

"She knows," Danny assured him. Lan liked Danny. He was funny and independent in a way that the kids of Andakar couldn't be. Not when any careless joke could bring the authorities to your door to haul you away.

Arriving at the third-floor landing, Lan walked to the rail and looked down. She hadn't seen her uncle since the night he caught her. She'd been terrified during their confrontation, but now the fear was gone. She was ready to face him.

"They're coming out," Kasey reported.

The cardigan and eyeglasses had been removed as Aung Win came back out. Her uncle motioned to someone inside. Ryan's mother appeared, squinting against the bright sunlight, her hands clasped together in front of her. Lan assumed the jacket draped over her wrists hid some kind of restraints. She recognized Kang, her uncle's oversized bodyguard who was never far from his side. Ryan's mom stumbled, wobbly on her feet, and Kang grabbed her arm to keep her from falling.

"Something's wrong with her." Ryan's voice was strained.

"She looks like she's been drugged," Kasey said, her tone reassuring. "They probably just gave her something to keep her calm. Stay focused, Ryan."

The driver opened the rear door. It was finally time for Lan to confront the man who had ruined her life.

"Uncle!"

Aung Win looked up at the third-story fire escape in astonishment. Lan stared down, both hands on the rail. Up here, she was far enough away to be safely out of reach, but close enough to see the uncertainty on his face.

"I know what you did. I know you were responsible for the car crash that killed my parents."

The guilty expression on Aung Win's face confirmed her suspicions. Only days before her uncle had caught her, Lan had accessed Aung Win's private emails and discovered several old messages arranging an "accidental" crash. She realized with horror that it was dated a week before her parents had died.

In an instant, she had understood. Her uncle had never had a family of his own. He had always been jealous of his brother's intelligent wife and energetic daughter. And so he had decided to make them his own. Only it didn't go as he had planned. Lan's mother wasn't supposed to be in the car that day. She wasn't supposed to die.

"That's absurd," Aung Win said. "Is that what this has all been about? It was an *accident*."

Lan saw that he had regained his composure. Her uncle was moving closer to the building.

"I found the emails. Proof that you murdered your own brother," Lan said to him.

"You're mistaken. Come down—let's talk about this. We're still family."

"No, I lost my family. And I'm going to make sure you lose everything you care about, too. I'm going to tell the world that *you're* Myat Kaw. And you know how easy it will be for them to believe me—because every secret I stole came from you!"

Lan headed back up the fire escape stairway. She had set the hook the best she could.

Now, if only her uncle took the bait.

CHAPTER

51

**NEW YORK,
USA**

ung Win's face twisted in rage. He noticed the ladder Ryan had unhooked earlier from the bottom of the fire escape. Bottom ladders were usually kept too high to reach from the street, but Ryan had lowered this one. And sure enough, Aung Win went for it, leaping up and pulling himself onto the rungs.

Lan slowed down at the stairs that led up to the next level. She needed to stay far enough ahead to not be caught, but close enough to keep her uncle in pursuit.

The distraction had worked. This was Ryan's chance.

When he'd first seen his mother, he'd been

momentarily overwhelmed. She was unsteady and disoriented, with dark circles under her eyes. And Lan's revelation that Aung Win was responsible for the deaths of her parents stunned him. But he couldn't afford to be sidetracked. He had to act fast.

Springing forward, he yelled, "Mom, duck!" Jacqueline reacted instantly, bending down. Ryan now had a clear shot at the bodyguard.

Ryan sprayed a stream of pepper spray right into the huge man's eyes! He screamed, hands covering his face, coughing and wheezing.

"Run!" Ryan yelled, grabbing his mom and pointing her down the street.

"Ryan, look out!" Jacqueline was looking over Ryan's shoulder. He spun around, raising the pepper spray. But the driver of the Town Car was too close. Before he could press the nozzle, the man batted his hand away, knocking the canister out of Ryan's grip. He punched Ryan in the stomach with enough force to make him double over, gasping.

The driver was about to strike again, when Jacqueline looped her hands around his neck and jerked him back. Her wrists were bound with plastic zip ties, which she now used as a weapon. His mom wasn't quite as drugged as she'd been pretending.

Ryan kicked the driver as hard as he could right in his crotch! The man's eyes opened wide, his cheeks puffed out, and he dropped to his knees. Mom knocked him out for good with a nasty kick to the side of the head. The body-guard was stumbling around, swinging blindly at whatever he heard. Ryan dodged a near hit, then grabbed his mom's hand, pulling her after him.

"Around the corner," he urged, trying to catch his breath.

Kasey ran to meet them. "Hold your hands up." Jacqueline did, and Kasey quickly snipped the ties with the wire cutters. "Come on, we have to meet the others at the car!"

Jacqueline turned to Ryan. "Is Dad here?"

"No."

"You did this on your own?"

"I got help from my friends." Ryan saw the driver was already shaking off the blow and back on his knees. "We have to go."

As they turned the corner, Ryan glanced back at the roof of the building, hoping the rest of the plan was working as well as this part did.

CHAPTER

52

**NEW YORK,
USA**

Danny leaned over the edge of the roof, watching anxiously as Lan dashed up the fire escape. Aung Win was close behind, quickly reducing the distance between them.

Danny could sense things turning bad. Aung Win was much faster than they'd guessed. Danny held a length of heavy pipe he'd found. He was ready to use it on Lan's crazy uncle if he had to.

"Hurry—he's catching up!" Danny shouted as she cleared the last set of stairs. Aung Win yelled at his niece and she glanced down. Lan's next step hit the rung of the ladder wrong. Her foot slid off the slick metal surface and she nearly fell. Aung Win leaped forward, grabbing for her ankle. But she dodged just in time, scrambling to the top where Danny hauled her over the edge.

"Get to Steeg," he said, turning back to the ladder with his heavy pipe. Time to play Whac-A-Mole on this dude's head!

But when Danny leaned over, he got a surprise: Aung Win had drawn his gun and was pointing it straight at him. Danny hurled the pipe as hard as he could. It slammed into Aung Win and knocked the gun from his hand. The weapon clattered along the fire escape, bouncing two levels down before coming to a rest. Aung Win roared with anger and surged upward.

Danny sprinted across the rooftop toward the office building next door, where it would be an easy drop from one building to the next. The plan was to make it to the office building's stairwell. Once they were inside, they could lock the metal door behind them and they'd be safe.

When Danny made it to the edge, Steeg was below, helping Lan drop from one roof down to the next. "Come on," Steeg urged, reaching up a hand to help Danny.

But before Danny could jump, Aung Win

shoved him. He toppled over, off-balance, and fell into Steeg. The boys tumbled to the ground. Danny rolled to his back and looked up as Aung Win loomed above them. The older man's eyes were poisonous as—*snit*—a switchblade snapped open in his hand.

"Move!" Lan yelled from the stairway door, which was propped open. Danny sprung to his feet and ran. As he closed the distance, he saw Lan looking in horror behind him. "Drew!" she screamed.

Danny stopped short, whirling around in time to see Aung Win leap down at Steeg. Steeg was big, but he was agile. He rolled out of the way as Aung Win landed. Crab crawling backward, he tried to get away, but a large air-conditioning unit blocked his way. Steeg was trapped as Aung Win advanced with the knife.

Danny charged at Aung Win with a ferocity he didn't know he possessed. He tackled the older man around the waist, trying to pull him down. But Aung Win was too strong. He stumbled, then quickly regained his balance and swung his knife.

Danny felt the blade slice his shoulder. He let go of Aung Win and staggered, stunned that he had actually been hit. His hand touched the wound and came away covered in blood.

Aung Win turned to Lan. "Do I need to kill them both?" he asked. Steeg tried to stand, but Aung Win's hand shot out, the point of the knife aimed right at the boy's chest. "Their blood will be on your hands . . . Myat Kaw."

Lan stepped forward, her face pale. "Let them go. You win, Uncle. I'll go with you."

"No," Steeg said.

Aung Win ignored him, striding toward her. "You will pay for your betrayal." He grabbed her roughly, pulling her through the stairwell door. The metal door slammed shut, locking Danny and Steeg out.

"We have to stop him," Steeg said, pulling out his cell phone.

"Yeah, we should . . . warn . . ." Danny's eyes fluttered before he fainted, collapsing to the roof.

CHAPTER

53

**NEW YORK,
USA**

"Danny's hurt." The panic in Steeg's voice was evident, even through the cell phone. "And Lan's gone—her uncle took her."

Ryan and Kasey locked eyes as she pressed the talk button: "Are you okay?"

"Yeah. I've got Danny. We're coming down the fire escape. There's a lot of blood."

Ryan looked at the Stieglitzes' Lexus, then turned to his mom. "Can you drive?"

Jacqueline shook her head, woozy. "I can barely focus."

"Kasey, call 911—tell them we need an ambulance," Ryan said, already running. He was thankful they'd rescued his mom, but knew that whatever happened to Danny or Lan was his fault.

Ryan rounded the corner just in time to see Aung Win forcing Lan into the back of the Town Car. "Hey, stop! Somebody help!" The street was mostly empty, but a couple walking a dog turned to stare as Ryan ran toward the car.

Aung Win got in and the car started moving even before the door was closed. The Town Car turned right at the intersection and disappeared around the corner. Ryan watched, helpless once again, as Aung Win sped off with someone he cared about.

"Put me down!" Danny's voice pulled Ryan's attention back to the fire escape. Steeg had the smaller boy thrown over his shoulder, using a fireman's carry to get him down the ladder.

"Shut up and keep still," Steeg said, grunting with each step. Ryan ran over and helped lower Danny the rest of the way to the pavement. Steeg had taken off his jacket and used one sleeve to tightly wrap Danny's wound. Both the jacket and Danny were caked with blood.

Ryan's stomach clenched, fearing the worst for his friend. "Aw, man, what did he do to you?"

But Danny shrugged it off. "It's not that deep. I'm just kind of a wimp about blood. I've fainted at the doctor's office a few times."

"You probably saved my life up there," Steeg said. "You're no wimp."

"Remember that the next time you want to stuff me in a locker." Danny turned to Ryan. "Lan's uncle is nuts. You have to go after her."

"We need to get you to a doctor first." Ryan glanced down the street, where Kasey and Jacqueline were approaching. "I should've never let Lan help. I knew it was too dangerous."

Danny grabbed Ryan's arm. "Lan could've saved herself—she had the chance. But she didn't. She went with her uncle to save *us*."

Jacqueline knelt on the other side of Danny. "Stay still, Danny—let me take a look." Even in her disoriented state, her movements were assured and efficient.

Danny's eyes never left Ryan's. He thrust his own cell phone into Ryan's hand. "The phone I gave Lan—it's got my tracking app on it."

Ryan looked at Danny's phone and realized what his friend meant. He jumped up, turning to Steeg. "Will you drive?"

Steeg was already moving. "Hell yeah."

Ryan pulled off the Roy Halladay–signed baseball cap and put it on Danny's head. "For luck," he said, then raced off after Steeg.

"Drew!" Kasey yelled after them.

Hearing the alarm in Kasey's voice, Jacqueline looked up. "Ryan, no!"

Around the corner, Ryan jumped into the passenger seat of the Lexus as Steeg fired up the engine. With screeching tires, the sedan took the corner without slowing. They raced off in pursuit of the Town Car.

CHAPTER
54

**NEW YORK,
USA**

S teeg floored it, cutting in and out of traffic. Approaching a stoplight just as it turned red, Steeg hit the gas and the Lexus shot through the intersection. Angry drivers honked, forced to brake abruptly.

"Please, god, do not let us pass any cops," Steeg said, veering around a slow truck in front of them and jetting forward.

"Try not to crash," Ryan said, glancing down at Danny's tracker app and setting it to find Lan's phone.

"Brilliant. Wish I'd thought of that." Steeg accelerated around two more vehicles, swerving in and out of lanes to find a clear path.

A blinking red heart appeared on the map.

Ryan grinned. Of course that's the symbol Danny would give Lan. Looking up, he pointed ahead.

"Left up here. They're not that far ahead."

At the corner, Steeg took the left. The boulevard contained a shifting sea of delivery trucks, yellow taxis, and cars. Ryan forced himself not to examine each individual vehicle, focusing instead only on the color black.

Finally, he caught sight of the Town Car turning at the next block. "There—Spring Street!"

Steeg was on the wrong side of Broadway and had to cut across two lanes of traffic to make the turn. Spring Street wasn't as busy, and Ryan could see that the Town Car was slowing to a stop at the next red light.

Ryan's phone buzzed and he saw Kasey's name pop up on his screen. Probably his mom calling to tell him to stop. He didn't have time to argue with her now, so he declined the call.

"What do we do if we catch them?" Steeg asked. "They've got guns."

Ryan hadn't actually thought that far ahead, simply moving on adrenaline. "We'll do what you said before. Follow them to wherever they're going and then call the cops."

Steeg glanced over. "I'm not sure how much

good that's gonna do."

"Why not?"

"Lan's still a teenager and her uncle's her legal guardian. Plus, he's got diplomatic immunity. There's nothing the cops can do except maybe give him a speeding ticket. If he wants to take her back to Andakar, the police can't stop him." As he narrowed the distance between the two cars, Steeg clutched the steering wheel tightly. "I should've stopped him. I let him take her."

"No, it's my fault. You guys were never even supposed to be that close to Aung Win. I thought you'd be gone long before he got to the roof."

They drove in silence, Ryan racking his brain for a way to save Lan. Steeg looked over at him. "I was a jerk to you and Danny at school," he said. "Sorry. You guys are okay."

"You were just looking out for your little sister. Protecting her."

"Yeah, that's probably what Lan's douchebag uncle says to himself, too. That he's just protecting his people, looking out for them. But he's really nothing but a bully." Steeg glanced over at Ryan. "I'm not like him."

Ryan was surprised by the conviction in his tone. "I never thought you were."

As they made their way across the Bowery, Steeg stayed close to the Town Car, keeping behind a brown UPS truck so they wouldn't be visible. The UPS truck abruptly shifted lanes, leaving the Lexus exposed. Ryan was shocked to see Aung Win turned around in his seat, looking out the back window right at them!

"He saw us," Ryan blurted, as the Town Car swerved hard to the right, taking off down a side street. Steeg pounded the brake, spinning the wheel so the sedan skidded into a turn. They fishtailed, but he managed to straighten out and keep going.

Now that they knew they were being followed, the driver of the Town Car was much more aggressive, weaving in and out of traffic. Steeg trailed behind, matching his moves, though he wasn't nearly as fast. The Town Car driver had obviously done this before.

"He's turning again," Ryan said. "Left—left!"

Steeg attempted the turn, but didn't quite make it, popping over the curb and hitting a green trash can next to the streetlight. The trash can smashed off the bumper as the Lexus bounced down the other side of the curb, heading right for a parked car. Steeg jerked the wheel, barely avoiding a collision.

"Man, I'm so gonna be grounded for this."

Ryan saw something fly out of the Town Car's back window. Almost instantly, the blinking red heart on the tracking app disappeared.

"He threw her phone out. Don't lose them!"

The Town Car executed a series of sharp turns. Steeg did his best to keep up, but he was no match for the professional driver, who clearly didn't care if he hit any pedestrians. After several minutes, the Lexus pulled into an intersection, Ryan looking one way, Steeg the other.

"Where'd they go?" Steeg asked.

"I didn't see." Ryan glanced down as his phone began buzzing once more. Kasey's ID again—probably his mom. He ignored it, searching the streets for the Town Car.

But it was gone.

Steeg pulled the Lexus to the curb. "What do we do now?"

Looking out the front window, Ryan noticed the metal towers of the Williamsburg Bridge in the distance. With all the erratic turns, he hadn't realized where they were. But as he looked at the sweeping expanse of the bridge that connected Manhattan to Long Island, something struck him: "When Aung Win called to set up the trade for my mom, he wanted to meet at the East Shore Aerodrome."

Gazing at the bridge, Steeg made the connection. "So they could have been coming this direction to get on the Williamsburg Bridge. But that place isn't a real airport, is it?"

"No. It's more of a club for people with old planes," Ryan said, feeling like he was on the right track. "But it's got a runway and lots of old hangars and buildings."

Steeg got it, already shifting the car back into gear. "A good place to hide a private jet."

"If he gets Lan on a plane, we'll never get her back."

Steeg said what they both feared: "If he hasn't killed her already."

CHAPTER

55

**NEW YORK,
USA**

Kasey hung up her phone, frustrated. She'd tried to call Ryan and Drew both, but neither had answered. The sidewalk was now busy with onlookers who were curious about all the excitement, and the sounds of sirens could be heard approaching. Things were about to get even more complicated.

Jacqueline had attended to Danny's cut with the proficiency of a field medic. She'd stripped off Drew's bloody jacket, and then appropriated a scarf and bottle of water from one of the bystanders to clean and bandage the wound. Despite her ordeal and the drugs in her system, Ryan's mom stayed focused. This was a woman used to handling a crisis, Kasey thought.

As the paramedics arrived, Jacqueline turned to Kasey. "Your bag," she said. "Do you have a hair band or any makeup?"

Kasey was surprised by the request. "I think I have both." Opening the bag, she pushed aside the scissors and tools, grabbing a scrunchie from the bottom and some blush and lip gloss from the zippered compartment.

Jacqueline pulled her disheveled hair into a ponytail and slid the scrunchie into place. As she applied the lip gloss and a quick dab of blush to her cheeks, she whispered urgently to Kasey. "Danny was robbed. The attacker was a white male in his twenties, wearing a green hoodie. He took off down the street. Got it?"

Kasey nodded, feeling like she was in a spy movie.

"Keep trying to reach Ryan." Jacqueline handed back the makeup as she stepped toward the arriving paramedics. "Thank goodness you're here! This poor boy says he was mugged, but I think he's okay."

Jacqueline's transformation was amazing, the weary victim replaced in a few moments with an energetic Good Samaritan. Kasey marveled at how quickly she had adapted to the situation.

Kasey stepped away from the crowd as Danny took to the story like a fish to water and hammed it up for the crowd: "I could've taken him, but he was huge—like, seven feet tall— maybe *bigger*!"

Instead of phoning Ryan again, she texted, *It's Kasey—call me!* Moments later, her phone vibrated, and she answered instantly. "Are you guys okay?"

"We lost Lan," Ryan said. "Sorry I didn't pick up. I thought it was my mom."

Kasey glanced over at Jacqueline, who was now busy with the paramedics as they checked out Danny. "She's got her hands full right now. Where are you?"

"Long Island. Headed toward the East Shore Aerodrome."

Kasey heard the frustration in Ryan's tone. "That's where Aung Win wanted to make the trade, right?"

"Yeah. I'm hoping maybe he has a plane hidden there."

"It makes sense he'd want to trade somewhere he could get her out of the country right away." Kasey thought of something else. "Remember that warehouse Danny and I investigated? They had all that top secret, high-tech equipment hidden away that they weren't supposed to have. Maybe a private plane is how they get it all out of the country."

"If Aung Win was caught smuggling top secret tech out of the United States, his diplomatic immunity could be stripped."

"I've got an idea," Kasey said, digging in her bag. She retrieved the business card Agent Calloway had given her, flipping it over to see the CIA agent's handwritten cell phone number on the back. Glancing over, she saw that Danny was being wheeled away on a gurney. "I gotta go—I'll call you back."

Without waiting for an answer, she hung up, pushing her way through to Danny. "Where are you going?"

"The hospital—but I'm fine. I just need a few stitches. Hopefully, I'll have an awesome scar."

Kasey leaned in close, walking along with the gurney. "I need the video of the warehouse."

Sensing her urgency, Danny pulled out a thin wallet and handed it over. "All the memory cards are in there. What's going on?"

"It's time we got a little help," Kasey told him. The paramedics hauled Danny up into the truck and slammed the doors closed.

Kasey dialed Agent Calloway's number.

CHAPTER
56

**NEW YORK,
USA**

A huge sign read East Shore Aerodrome—
Aviation Historical Society. Below that
was another sign: No Trespassing!

"Looks deserted," Steeg said.

Ryan got out of the Lexus to take a look. The
afternoon was turning into evening, twilight
coming on quickly. Tall trees lined the fence in
both directions. On the other side of the gate,
the road veered off to the right, making it impossible to see the actual airfield.

The gate was wrapped with chains and
locked up tight. Ryan checked to see if he could
climb the fence, but the top was lined with
barbed wire. Steeg got out and followed as
Ryan left the road and walked the property line.

He hoped to find a spot where he could see the runway or possibly find a tree to climb.

"Maybe he took her somewhere else," Steeg suggested.

Then, a high-pitched whine echoed through the trees. They froze in place, listening.

"That sounds like a plane," Ryan said.

Steeg pivoted and ran for the Lexus. "They're gonna take off!"

Ryan dashed after him, getting in the passenger seat just as Steeg shifted into reverse. He backed the car up several feet, then slammed into drive. "Hold on!"

Ryan grabbed the handhold above him, bracing himself as the car surged forward. They hit the entrance with a violent impact, snapping the lock and flinging the gates wide open!

Inside, the road changed from asphalt to dirt. They still couldn't see the runway because of the surrounding trees, but the sound of the plane's engine was getting closer.

"Stop here," Ryan said. "We don't want them to see us."

Steeg pulled to the side of the road and they both got out. Using the trees as cover, they crept forward until they had a view of the airfield.

A collection of hangars and small buildings

ran alongside a grass runway, which stretched off into the distance. Halfway down, one of the hangars was open and a sleek, private jet emerged into the twilight.

"They're here." Ryan pointed to the Town Car, parked just outside the hangar. The bodyguard and driver stood watching the jet as it taxied forward.

"If they get her in that plane," Steeg said, "she's gone forever."

Ryan noticed an old bi-wing plane, like something the Red Baron would have flown, tethered close to one of the sheet metal structures. The vintage plane was probably part of the historical society mentioned on the sign. Looking past it, he realized that the buildings along the runway formed a line. From the airfield, it would be impossible to see the road.

"We can drive around behind the hangars," he said. "They won't be able to see your car from the runway. If we come up between the buildings, we might be able to surprise them."

"And then what? What exactly is our play here?"

"Kinda making it up as I go along," Ryan admitted.

Steeg shook his head. "How did I end up taking directions from an *eighth grader*?"

They hurried back to the car and Steeg drove behind the row of buildings, where they couldn't be seen. As they approached the hangar with the jet, the whine of the engine drowned out all other sound. Steeg got as close to the back of the hangar as possible before Ryan stopped him and jumped out. "Wait here."

Ryan ran to the front of the hangar and peered around the corner. The jet was very close, a small but stylish private plane. The stairs were down, and two cargo doors in the back were now open. The bodyguard and the driver helped the pilot and two other men load crates. Ryan recognized the logo of LTV Technologies from the video Kasey and Danny had taken at the warehouse. Aung Win was smuggling the stolen, top secret technology out of the country on the same flight he was taking with Lan.

The back door of the Town Car opened and Aung Win got out, giving orders to his men. He gestured impatiently as Lan slid across the seat. Aung Win motioned for her to get on the plane, and she began to shuffle forward slowly. Ryan darted back to the open passenger window of the Lexus.

"They're putting her on the jet," he said. "Can

you keep them busy?"

"What're you gonna do?"

"I'm gonna get her out of there."

Steeg peeled out, lying on the horn as he zoomed by. The Lexus exploded from between the hangars and headed right for the jet! Steeg was driving like he was insane.

Ryan sprinted, knowing he'd only have seconds before Aung Win spotted him. Up ahead, Aung Win and Lan dodged out of the way as the sedan swerved back and forth. The huge bodyguard was already drawing a gun as Steeg steered right toward him.

The Lexus plowed into the open door of the Town Car, wrenching it off its hinges. The body-guard tried to jump from its path, but he was too slow. The Lexus clipped his legs—he rolled over the hood before crashing to the ground.

"Lan!" Ryan closed the distance as she looked up, shocked to see him there. "This way!"

Lan reacted a moment too late, giving her uncle time to grab her. He pulled her close, but was caught off guard when she slammed the back of her skull right into his jaw! Aung Win shrieked in agony, letting go. Lan shoved him away and took off running.

Ryan indicated the dark hangars. "In there!"

As they ran, he glanced back. Steeg was spinning the Lexus around to come back for them. But the Town Car driver fired a shot, shattering the Lexus's side window. Ryan froze—did the bullet hit Steeg? But the Lexus did a quick U-turn, letting him know Steeg was still driving. Another shot rang out, forcing him to speed off away from the hangars.

Ryan made it to the hangar as Lan disappeared inside. Aung Win and the driver were coming after them, guns drawn and closing in fast.

CHAPTER
57

**NEW YORK,
USA**

Inside, the hangar was cavernous and dark. It must be some kind of maintenance area, Ryan thought. It was crammed with racks full of airplane parts and tools. He and Lan ducked behind a tall, mobile staircase used by mechanics to reach the airplane engines.

"You shouldn't have come after me," Lan whispered. "He'll kill you, too."

"Only if he catches us," Ryan said.

Ryan took her hand and they ran behind a row of steel shelves, crouching low to keep out of sight. The door to the hangar burst open. Aung Win and the driver entered, their raised weapons silhouetted against the evening sky. They split up, the driver moving away while

Aung Win came in their direction.

Spread across the length of the hangar were three vintage planes; two were bi-wings like the one outside, and the other was a Piper Cub with a big propeller on its front. Ryan motioned toward the Piper Cub, and Lan moved that way. Passing a rolling metal tool chest, Ryan had an idea. He grabbed the first thing he found—a screwdriver sitting right on top—and hurled it across the hangar.

The screwdriver hit the far side of the building with a loud bang. Aung Win fired instantly, the sound echoing in the confined space. He headed off in search of Ryan and Lan, as they continued in the opposite direction.

"I think I see an exit." Lan pointed to the far corner of the hangar, which was mostly lost in shadows. The faint outline of a door was barely visible.

"All right," Ryan whispered. "Halfway there."

The clatter of a screw skittering across the concrete caused Ryan to swivel around. The driver was right behind them! Ryan pulled Lan out of the way as another shot rang out. Before the driver could fire again, Ryan was on him, using his forearms like a battering ram to knock the wiry man down.

"Get to the door," Ryan said. He turned to follow Lan, but the driver grabbed his leg, tripping him. He fell, the driver on top of him before he knew what was happening. The guy was fast, straddling Ryan and wrapping both hands around his throat. Ryan gasped, but he couldn't get any air, the driver choking him viciously, trying to crush his windpipe.

Wham! Lan swung a wrench into the side of the driver's head and he toppled over, out cold before he even hit the floor. With a fierce look in her eyes, she reached out to give Ryan a hand up. "Let's get out of here."

"So brave." They both whirled around to discover Aung Win, his pistol aimed at Lan's head. "But so stupid. Did you think two children could outwit a colonel of the ASI?"

Ryan stepped in front of Lan, instinctively shielding her. Aung Win scrutinized him, curious. "Why do you care? Why risk so much for someone you barely know?"

Ryan met his gaze head-on. "Call it a family tradition."

"In the end, Myat Kaw is nothing but one sad little voice against the power of Andakar's generals."

"Well, she certainly scared you," Ryan said.

"When she's gone, no one will remember she ever existed."

"Then someone new will step up to take my place," Lan said, defiantly. "There'll always be someone to stand up to tyrants like you."

Annoyed, Aung Win stepped forward, raising his gun . . . but then, hearing something, he hesitated. It was the roar of a helicopter outside, getting closer by the moment.

"This is the FBI," a voice from a bullhorn bellowed. "Lay down your weapons and lie on the ground!" Confused, Aung Win looked to Ryan.

"Sounds like they're talking to your men," Ryan said. "But I think *you're* the one they really want."

Aung Win sneered. "Your FBI and police can't touch me. I have diplomatic immunity."

"You also have a plane full of stolen top secret military technology sitting on the runway." Ryan saw Aung Win's bravado falter. "That's espionage. Immunity won't protect you."

Aung Win couldn't disguise his panic as the reality of his situation set in.

"Lower your weapons immediately!" the bullhorn thundered once more. Aung Win involuntarily glanced toward the door and Ryan sprang forward, knowing this might be his only chance.

He grabbed Aung Win's wrist, jerking his arm straight up as Aung Win fired. The blast so close to his ear was disorienting, but Ryan managed to rip the gun from Aung Win's grasp, knocking it away. Ryan tried driving an elbow into Aung Win's stomach, but the older man was too fast. He ducked the blow and punched Ryan hard in the small of the back.

Ryan stumbled as Lan charged, the wrench held high. Her uncle easily sidestepped the attack, using Lan's own momentum to send her sprawling onto the concrete. Turning to Ryan, Aung Win produced the switchblade. The knife flicked open in his hand.

"You should have just given me the traitor." Aung Win lunged, the blade barely missing Ryan as he twisted out of reach. He took off running, hoping to lure Lan's uncle away so she could escape. But within a few feet, he realized he couldn't outpace Aung Win.

Changing direction, Ryan sprinted toward the bi-plane. As Aung Win reached him, Ryan dropped into a slide, gliding on the smooth concrete floor underneath the plane's body. It bought him a few seconds, as Aung Win had to go around.

As he ran, Ryan's shoulder grazed a tall metal

rack filled with airplane parts, and it swayed, pieces falling to the floor. On the top shelf, a small propeller rattled precariously, giving Ryan an idea. He backed up to the corner of the rack, waiting.

Aung Win came around, stopping as he spotted Ryan. Ryan grabbed the edge of the rack and pulled with everything he had. The propeller tumbled off the top shelf and hit Aung Win's head. The rest of the rack followed as Ryan brought the entire thing crashing down, pinning Aung Win underneath!

As Aung Win moaned, Ryan came around and stared down at him. "That's for my mom."

"Ryan, come on!" Lan yelled.

Ryan glanced once more at Aung Win, who was stunned and immobile, then joined Lan across the hangar. They made it to the far door, exiting just as the FBI stormed in. They surrounded Aung Win, taking him into federal custody.

CHAPTER

58

LOCATION
UNKNOWN

Tasha didn't like the man in the bow tie. But he was a necessary evil. She had learned that you don't always have to like the people you work for.

And he did pay well.

The room they were using was dark and dingy, but the smell of sea salt in the air made it almost bearable. Hopefully, they wouldn't be here long. Just long enough to get the information they needed.

John Quinn struggled against the leather cuffs that secured him to the chair. It was probably a good thing he was gagged, Tasha thought. Based on the hate-filled glare he was giving her, she didn't want to hear anything he had to say.

"This will be easier if you don't resist," said the man in the bow tie. He was short and bald with pale skin. People who met him often guessed he was a professor, timid and brainy. But Tasha had learned not to underestimate him. The man in the bow tie was the most dangerous person she had ever met.

He held up a syringe with a thin needle. "Sodium thiopental. Commonly called truth serum. But this is my own formula—I think you'll find it's quite effective."

Quinn thrashed harder against the cuffs. But it did him no good. He wasn't getting away.

"You're going to give us names," the man in the bow tie told him. "That doesn't sound too difficult, does it? Names, addresses, contact information. And the best part is, when we're done—you won't remember a thing. Two days from now, you'll be back home with your family. Safe and sound with no memory whatsoever of what went on here."

John Quinn went still. He had finally realized what was happening. The Emergency Rescue Committee was about to be destroyed. And he was the one who would bring it down.

Quinn looked to Tasha, begging her with his eyes not to let this happen. But it was too late to turn back now.

The man in the bow tie turned to her. "I think it's time you made the call. We don't want his family to worry. Tell them he'll be home soon."

Tasha took out her phone and dialed. She turned away. The betrayal in John's eyes made her uncomfortable. Thankfully, her call was quickly answered.

"Tasha?" said Jacqueline Quinn, miles away in America.

"Jacqueline—thank goodness! Are you all right?"

"I am now. Are you with John?"

"Yes," Tasha said. "We made it across the border. He's with the doctors, but they're fixing him up. He's going to be fine."

Behind her, John Quinn roared beneath his gag. But it only lasted a few seconds. After that, there was silence.

CHAPTER
59

**NEW YORK,
USA**

Ryan finally got to hug his mom.

They held on for a long time, knowing how close they had come to losing each other. Finally, Jacqueline pulled away, smiling.

"Dad's okay. He's out of Andakar."

Ryan couldn't believe it. "He called?"

"Tasha Levi did. She found him and helped him cross the border."

"She made it!"

"Tasha can be challenging, but she's tough. They're in Thailand now. Dad was in surgery for his wound, but Tasha says he'll be out soon and he's doing well. They'll fly home tomorrow or the day after."

Ryan turned to Lan, just getting out of the

banged-up Lexus at the curb of the brownstone. "My dad got away," he told her. "You did it—you saved him."

He'd never seen Lan smile so brightly. She hugged him with relief as Steeg joined them on the sidewalk.

"Mom, this is Lan," Ryan said, as they parted.

"I know exactly who she is." Jacqueline took Lan's hands in her own. "You're a courageous young woman. We're going to do everything we can to help you."

"Your family's already done too much."

Ryan looked up at Kasey on the brownstone's front steps. "How's Danny?"

"Loving the attention. He'll probably be on every evening newscast before he's done. I think it's now up to four muggers that he single-handedly fought off."

Ryan laughed. Steeg just shook his head.

"Happy to see you're feeling better, Ryan." They all turned to discover Agent Calloway. Ryan and his mom instinctively moved closer together. "Have to say, you both look like you've been through quite an ordeal."

Her gaze was piercing, but Jacqueline didn't miss a beat. "Is there something we can help you with, agent?"

"I just came to say thanks." She turned to Kasey. "I thought I might find you here. We were so appreciative to get that video you sent."

"I'm happy to help," Kasey said without any hesitation. "It was pure luck I happened to go into that particular warehouse."

"With your camera running," Calloway added. "Very lucky."

"Sometimes things just work out." Ryan had to keep himself from grinning. Kasey was playing it so cool.

"Our associates at the FBI caught Aung Win and his men red-handed. And the Andakar military leadership is denying all knowledge of his activities. So he'll be going away for a long time." She suddenly focused on Lan. "And who are you?"

"Emma Manado," Lan said, using the name on her fake passport. "I'm visiting."

"She's a foreign exchange student," Jacqueline offered.

"From Indonesia," Ryan said. "She'll be staying with us awhile."

They were a united front. Agent Calloway nodded, looking at each in turn, letting them know she didn't believe them for a second. "Well, welcome to America, Emma Manado. I hope you like it here." She looked at Jacqueline. "I'll be anxious to talk to your husband when he returns. We still have a lot of questions."

She turned and walked off.

"Man, I don't know how much of this I can take," Steeg said. "I thought playing for the junior varsity championship was intense. But it's nothing compared to this."

Ryan grabbed his shoulder. "You kidding? You were awesome out there tonight."

"It *was* pretty exciting." He turned to the Lexus. "Though I don't think my dad's gonna be nearly as stoked."

"Don't worry about the car," Jacqueline said. "We'll get it fixed, along with a good cover story for your father."

Ryan turned to Kasey. "We better hurry or we're not gonna make it."

She was confused. "Make it where?"

"The Autumn Carnival Dance—it starts at eight, right?"

"Ryan, I was just kidding earlier," Kasey said. "We don't have to go—not after everything that's happened."

"I want to go. Lan's free, my parents are safe, and we just pulled off the craziest idea I've ever had in my life. Tonight, I just want to be a normal kid and go to my very first school dance." He turned to his mom. "If that's okay?"

"I think it sounds like a great idea."

Kasey looked down at her shirt and jeans. "Well, I can't go looking like this." She headed for the car, grabbing Steeg. "You've got to get me home to change!"

Steeg looked to Lan, nervous. "I don't— I mean, this is probably weird, but . . . if you wanted to—"

Ryan smiled as the big jock fumbled, then saved him. "I think what he's saying is, how'd you like to go to the dance with him?"

"Yeah." Steeg nodded. "What he said."

Lan was excited. "I've never danced with a boy."

"We don't have to dance if you don't want to."

"Oh, I want to!" They both had those goofy grins again.

Kasey opened the door for Lan. "Then get in—I've got the perfect dress for you to borrow." Lan climbed in as Steeg hurried to the driver's side. Kasey got in and slammed the door, then looked at Ryan. "See you soon."

As the Lexus raced off, Jacqueline put her arm around Ryan.

"I'm so proud of you. I hope you know that."

Ryan still felt some resentment about his parents' lifelong deception, but there'd be time to work through that later. "I'm just glad everybody's okay."

"We'll have a long talk when Dad gets home. There are things you need to know. But tonight, just have fun. Be a teenager—you deserve it."

Ryan had a feeling there was something else bothering his mother, something other than the Emergency Rescue Committee and its work. But for tonight, he was gonna take her advice and not worry about it.

Tonight, he was gonna have fun.

EPILOGUE

**NEW YORK,
USA**

The Autumn Carnival Dance was a riot of yellow and orange, with streamers draped everywhere and pumpkin-shaped paper lanterns suspended from the school cafeteria's ceiling. The floor was covered with countless red-and-gold maple leaf cutouts, giving Ryan the impression he was walking on a forest floor.

The party had been in full swing for a while now as he entered, a bass beat thumping and kids dancing to a hip-hop song Ryan didn't recognize. He searched the crowd and spotted Kasey, already heading toward him.

"You look incredible!" she said, taking in his new clothes. Ryan wore a sleek black blazer with gray skinny jeans and cherry-red high-tops.

"I didn't have much time to shop," he admitted. "Mom helped me pick everything out. Except for the high-tops—those were all me."

"Well, you've got excellent taste."

"That's what I kept telling her." Kasey laughed as Ryan admired her dress, a shimmering, silver, 1920s flapper style, with fringe that sparkled as it moved. "Wow. You're like a disco ball."

Kasey twirled, the fringe flaring and creating little flashes of light. "This was my costume for a musical production of *The Great Gatsby* last year. I know it's kind of gaudy, but I love it."

"It's perfect," Ryan said, totally meaning it.

"They're cute together." Kasey nodded across the room, where Lan clung to Steeg's arm, both of them dressed up now and looking great. Steeg was over a foot taller than Lan and held her close, protective as she marveled at the dancing kids, the loud music, and all the decorations.

Ryan understood how strange and bewildering this all must be for her—it still felt that way to him a lot of the time. But the truth was, kids around the world weren't actually all that different. They just wanted the freedom to be themselves, whoever that might be.

"Have you seen Danny?" Ryan asked.

"This way." She took his hand, leading him through the crowd. "Your mom made him a hero."

They found Danny sitting on a cafeteria table that had been pushed to the wall, surrounded by guys and girls, all listening with rapt attention. His arm was bandaged and hung in a sling around his neck.

"The guy was trying to rob this little old lady and I was like, 'Dude, back off, or I will take you down!'" Ryan smiled as Danny acted out his story. "So I'm all ready to do some karate on him, and then he pulls out this machete!"

"A machete?" Ryan said.

"Ry-ry!" Danny winked at a pretty girl who was smiling at him, then joined Ryan and Kasey. "Today was *so* worth five stitches."

Ryan laughed—Danny's enthusiasm was infectious. "Apparently."

"So what happens next? Are we, like, official members of the ERC now? Do we get to go rescue people and stuff?"

"I don't know." Ryan looked to Kasey, too. "All I know is, working together we managed to do something that none of us could have accomplished alone. So, thanks."

"Enough shop talk, boys. We came here to dance!" With a playful grin, Kasey beckoned them both to the dance floor. Danny followed, already grooving, even with his arm in a sling.

Ryan was nervous. Would he look like an idiot trying to dance with all these kids who knew what they were doing? He took a deep breath, telling himself to just get it over with, when Principal Milankovic stepped in front of him.

"Mr. Quinn. It's good to see you're feeling well again."

"Oh, uh—yeah. Thanks." Principal Milankovic wore a stern expression, and Ryan could tell he was skeptical. "I'll be sure to bring a note from my parents on Monday."

The principal nodded, his attitude softening. "I'm glad you're okay. I was worried."

"Thanks." There was something odd in his manner, Ryan thought, like it was personal to him. But Ryan had known Milankovic for only the past couple of months. Shaking off the weird feeling, he started toward the dance floor, when the principal suddenly grabbed his elbow, stopping him.

"You have to talk to your parents," he whispered urgently. He looked up, scanning the room as if to make sure no one was watching them. "There's so much you don't know."

"About what?"

"It's not my place to say. But you deserve the truth." Now, he looked Ryan right in the eye. "The truth about who you really are. Ask your parents."

Abruptly, Principal Milankovic let go and walked away. He strode off through the crowd, leaving Ryan confused.

What did he mean, the truth about who you really are?

Ryan started to go after him, but Kasey was suddenly at his side, taking his hand.

"Come on," she encouraged. "It's not that scary!"

Ryan glanced toward Milankovic's retreating figure but finally allowed her to lead him toward the dance floor. A sea of dancing teenagers quickly engulfed him.

"It's okay to let go," Kasey shouted over the music. "It's all over now."

Ryan knew in his heart it wasn't over at all. In fact, this felt more like a beginning. But she was right. For tonight, everyone was home and life was good again.

So Ryan made himself forget about what might be ahead and focus on where he was right now. He knew he wasn't a very good dancer, but that didn't seem to matter much. Surrounded by his friends, Ryan finally let loose, the music and laughter washing over him, and, for a little while at least, life was perfect.

TO BE CONTINUED . . .